Prince Zaleski and
Cummings King Monk

M. P. SHIEL

Prince Zaleski
and
Cummings King Monk

Mycroft & Moran
Sauk City • Wisconsin

International Standard Book Number 0-87054-007-6
Library of Congress Catalog Card Number 76-17993

Frontispiece design by Bob Arrington.

Contents

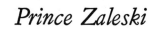

Prince Zaleski

The Race of Orven

Never without grief and pain could I remember the fate of Prince Zaleski — victim of a too importunate, too unfortunate Love, which the fulgor of the throne itself could not abash; exile perforce from his native land, and voluntary exile from the rest of men! Having renounced the world, over which, lurid and inscrutable as a falling star, he had passed, the world quickly ceased to wonder at him; and even I, to whom, more than to another, the workings of that just and passionate mind had been revealed, half forgot him in the rush of things.

But during the time that what was called the "Pharanx labyrinth" was exercising many of the heaviest brains in the land, my thought turned repeatedly to him; and even when the affair had passed from the general attention, a bright day in spring, combined perhaps with a latent mistrust of the *dénoûment* of that dark plot, drew me to his place of hermitage.

I reached the gloomy abode of my friend as the sun set. It was a vast palace of the older world standing lonely in the midst of woodland, and approached by a somber avenue of poplars and cypresses, through which the sunlight hardly pierced. Up this I passed, and seeking out the deserted stables (which I found all too dilapidated to afford shelter) finally put up my *calèche* in the ruined sacristy of an old Dominican chapel, and turned my mare loose to browse for the night on a paddock behind the domain.

As I pushed back the open front door and entered the mansion,

I could not but wonder at the saturnine fancy that had led this wayward man to select a brooding-place so desolate for the passage of his days. I regarded it as a vast tomb of Mausolus in which lay deep sepulchered how much genius, culture, brilliancy, power! The hall was constructed in the manner of a Roman *atrium,* and from the oblong pool of turgid water in the center a troop of fat and otiose rats fled weakly squealing at my approach. I mounted by broken marble steps to the corridors running round the open space, and thence pursued my way through a mazeland of apartments — suite upon suite — along many a length of passage, up and down many stairs. Dust-clouds rose from the uncarpeted floors and choked me; incontinent Echo coughed answering *ricochets* to my footsteps in the gathering darkness, and added emphasis to the funereal gloom of the dwelling. Nowhere was there a vestige of furniture — nowhere a trace of human life.

After a long interval I came, in a remote tower of the building and near its utmost summit, to a richly-carpeted passage, from the ceiling of which three mosaic lamps shed dim violet, scarlet, and pale-rose lights around. At the end I perceived two figures standing as if in silent guard on each side of a door tapestried with the python's skin. One was a post-replica in Parian marble of the nude Aphrodite of Cnidus; in the other I recognized the gigantic form of the negro Ham, the prince's only attendant, whose fierce, and glistening, and ebon visage broadened into a grin of intelligence as I came nearer. Nodding to him, I pushed without ceremony into Zaleski's apartment.

The room was not a large one, but lofty. Even in the semi-darkness of the very faint greenish luster radiated from an open censerlike *lampas* of fretted gold in the center of the domed encausted roof, a certain incongruity of barbaric gorgeousness in the furnishing filled me with amazement. The air was heavy with the scented odor of this light, and the fumes of the narcotic *cannabis sativa* — the base of the *bhang* of the Mohammedans — in which I knew it to be the habit of my friend to assuage himself. The hangings were of wine-colored velvet, heavy, gold-fringed and embroidered at Nurshedabad. All the world knew Prince Zaleski to be a consummate *cognoscente* — a profound amateur — as well as a savant and a thinker; but I was, nevertheless, astounded at the mere multitudinousness of the curios he had contrived to crowd into the space around him. Side by side rested a palaeolithic implement, a Chinese "wise man," a Gnostic gem, an amphora of Graeco-Etruscan work. The general effect was a *bizarrerie* of half-weird sheen and gloom. Flemish sepulchral brasses companied strangely with runic tablets, miniature paintings, a winged bull, Tamil scriptures on lacquered leaves of the talipot, mediaeval reliquaries richly gemmed, Brahmin gods. One whole side of the room was occupied by an organ whose thunder in that circumscribed place must have set all these relics of dead epochs clashing and jingling in fantastic dances. As I entered, the vaporous atmosphere was palpitating to the low, liquid tinkling of an invisible musical box. The prince reclined on a couch from which a draping of cloth-of-silver rolled torrent over the floor. Beside him, stretched in its open sarcophagus which rested on three brazen trestles, lay the mummy of an ancient Memphian, from the upper part of which the brown cerements had rotted or been rent, leaving the hideousness of the naked, grinning countenance exposed to view.

Discarding his gemmed chibouque and an old vellum reprint of Anacreon, Zaleski rose hastily and greeted me with warmth, muttering at the same time some commonplace about his "pleasure" and the "unexpectedness" of my visit. He then gave orders to Ham to prepare me a bed in one of the adjoining chambers. We passed the greater part of the night in a delightful stream of that somnolent and half-mystic talk which Prince Zaleski alone could initiate and sustain, during which he repeatedly pressed on me a concoction of Indian hemp resembling *hashish,* prepared by his own hands, and quite innocuous. It was after a simple breakfast the next morning that I entered on the subject which was partly the occasion of my visit. He lay back on his couch, volumed in a Turkish *beneesh,* and listened to me, a little wearily perhaps at first, with woven fingers, and the pale inverted eyes of old anchorites and astrologers, the moony greenish light falling on his always wan features.

"You knew Lord Pharanx?" I asked.

"I have met him in 'the world.' His son Lord Randolph, too, I saw once at Court at Peterhof, and once again at the Winter Palace of the Tsar. I noticed in their great stature, shaggy heads of hair, ears of a very peculiar conformation, and a certain aggressiveness of demeanor — a strong likeness between father and son."

I had brought with me a bundle of old newspapers, and comparing these as I went on, I proceeded to lay the incidents before him.

"The father," I said, "held, as you know, high office in a late Administration, and was one of our big luminaries in politics; he has also been President of the Council of several learned societies, and author of a book on modern ethics. His son was rapidly rising to eminence in the *corps diplomatique,* and lately (though, strictly speaking, *unebenbürtig*) contracted an affiance with the Prinzessin Charlotte Mariana Natalia of Morgen-üppigen, a lady with a strain of indubitable Hohenzollern blood in her royal veins. The Orven family is a very old and distinguished one, though — especially in modern days — far from wealthy. However, some little time after Randolph had become engaged to this royal lady, the father insured his life for immense sums in various offices both in England and America, and the reproach of poverty is now swept from the race. Six months ago, almost simultaneously, both father and son resigned their various positions *en bloc.* But all this, of course, I am telling you on the assumption that you have not already read it in the papers.''

''A modern newspaper,'' he said, ''being what it mostly is, is the one thing insupportable to me at present. Believe me, I never see one.''

''Well, then, Lord Pharanx, as I said, threw up his posts in the fullness of his vigor, and retired to one of his country seats. A good many years ago, he and Randolph had a terrible row over some trifle, and, with the implacability that distinguishes their race, had not since exchanged a word. But some little time after the retirement of the father, a message was despatched by him to the son, who was then in India. Considered as the first step in the *rapprochement* of this proud and selfish pair of beings, it was an altogether remarkable message, and was subsequently deposed to in evidence by a telegraph official; it ran:

'''*Return. The beginning of the end is come.*' Whereupon Randolph did return, and in three months from the date of his landing in England, Lord Pharanx was dead.''

''*Murdered?*''

A certain something in the tone in which this word was ut-

tered by Zaleski puzzled me. It left me uncertain whether he had
addressed to me an exclamation of conviction, or a simple
question. I must have looked this feeling, for he said at once:

"I could easily, from your manner, surmise as much, you
know. Perhaps I might even have foretold it, years ago."

"Foretold — what? Not the murder of Lord Pharanx?"

"Something of that kind," he answered with a smile; "but
proceed — tell me all the facts you know."

Word-mysteries of this sort fell frequent from the lips of the
prince. I continued the narrative.

"The two, then, met, and were reconciled. But it was a
reconciliation without cordiality, without affection — a shaking
of hands across a barrier of brass; and even this hand-shaking was
a strictly metaphorical one, for they do not seem ever to have
got beyond the interchange of a frigid bow. The opportunities,
however, for observation were few. Soon after Randolph's
arrival at Orven Hall, his father entered on a life of the most absolute seclusion. The mansion is an old three-storied one, the
top floor consisting for the most part of sleeping-rooms, the first
of a library, drawing-room, and so on, and the ground-floor, in
addition to the dining and other ordinary rooms, of another
small library, looking out (at the side of the house) on a low
balcony, which, in turn, looks on a lawn dotted with flowerbeds. It was this smaller library on the ground-floor that was
now divested of its books, and converted into a bedroom for the
earl. Hither he migrated, and here he lived, scarcely ever leaving
it. Randolph, on his part, moved to a room on the first floor immediately above this. Some of the retainers of the family were
dismissed, and on the remaining few fell a hush of expectancy, a
sense of wonder, as to what these things boded. A great enforced

quiet pervaded the building, the least undue noise in any part being sure to be followed by the angry voice of the master demanding the cause. Once, as the servants were supping in the kitchen on the side of the house most remote from that which he occupied, Lord Pharanx, slippered and in dressing-gown, appeared at the doorway, purple with rage, threatening to pack the whole company of them out of doors if they did not moderate the clatter of their knives and forks. He had always been regarded with fear in his own household, and the very sound of his voice now became a terror. His food was taken to him in the room he had made his habitation, and it was remarked that, though simple before in his gustatory tastes, he now — possibly owing to the sedentary life he led — became fastidious, insisting on *recherché* bits. I mention all these details to you — as I shall mention others — not because they have the least connection with the tragedy as it subsequently occurred, but merely because I know them, and you have requested me to state all I know.''

''Yes,'' he answered, with a suspicion of *ennui,* ''you are right. I may as well hear the whole — if I must hear a part.''

''Meanwhile, Randolph appears to have visited the earl at least once a day. In such retirement did he, too, live that many of his friends still supposed him to be in India. There was only one respect in which he broke through this privacy. You know, of course, that the Orvens are, and, I believe, always have been, noted as the most obstinate, the most crabbed of Conservatives in politics. Even among the past-enamored families of England, they stand out conspicuously in this respect. Is it credible to you, then, that Randolph should offer himself to the Radical Association of the Borough of Orven as a candidate for the next election in opposition to the sitting member? It is on record, too, that he spoke at three public meetings — reported in local papers — at which he avowed his political conversion; afterwards laid the foundation-stone of a new Baptist chapel; presided at a Methodist tea-meeting; and taking an abnormal interest in the debased condition of the laborers in the villages round, fitted up as a classroom an apartment on the top floor at Orven Hall, and gathered round him on two evenings in every week a class of yokels, whom he proceeded to cram with demonstrations in elementary mechanics.''

"Mechanics!" cried Zaleski, starting upright for a moment, "mechanics to agricultural laborers! Why not elementary chemistry? Why not elementary botany? *Why* mechanics?"

This was the first evidence of interest he had shown in the story. I was pleased, but answered:

"The point is unimportant; and there really is no accounting for the vagaries of such a man. He wished, I imagine, to give some idea to the young illiterates of the simple laws of motion and force. But now I come to a new character in the drama — the chief character of all. One day a woman presented herself at Orven Hall and demanded to see its owner. She spoke English with a strong French accent. Though approaching middle life she was still beautiful, having wild black eyes, and creamy-pale face. Her dress was tawdry, cheap, and loud, showing signs of wear; her hair was unkempt; her manners were not the manners of a lady. A certain vehemence, exasperation, unrepose distinguished all she said and did. The footman refused her admission; Lord Pharanx, he said, was invisible. She persisted violently, pushed past him, and had to be forcibly ejected; during all which the voice of the master was heard roaring from the passage red-eyed remonstrance at the unusual noise. She went away gesticulating wildly, and vowing vengeance on Lord Pharanx and all the world. It was afterwards found that she had taken up her abode in one of the neighboring hamlets, called Lee.

"This person, who gave the name of Maude Cibras, subsequently called at the Hall three times in succession, and was each time refused admittance. It was now, however, thought advisable to inform Randolph of her visits. He said she might be permitted to see him, if she returned. This she did on the next day, and had a long interview in private with him. Her voice was heard raised as if in angry protest by one Hester Dyett, a servant of the house, while Randolph in low tones seemed to try to soothe her. The conversation was in French, and no word could be made out. She passed out at length, tossing her head jauntily, and smiling a vulgar triumph at the footman who had before opposed her ingress. She was never known to seek admission to the house again.

"But her connection with its inmates did not cease. The same Hester asserts that one night, coming home late through the park, she saw two persons conversing on a bench beneath the trees, crept behind some bushes, and discovered that they were the strange woman and Randolph. The same servant bears evidence to tracking them to other meeting-places, and to finding in the letter-bag letters addressed to Maude Cibras in Randolph's handwriting. One of these was actually unearthed later on. Indeed, so engrossing did the intercourse become, that it seems even to have interfered with the outburst of radical zeal in the new political convert. The *rendezvous* — always held under cover of darkness, but naked and open to the eye of the watchful Hester — sometimes clashed with the science lectures, when these latter would be put off, so that they became gradually fewer, and then almost ceased.''

''Your narrative becomes unexpectedly interesting,'' said Zaleski; ''but this unearthed letter of Randolph's — what was in it?''

I read as follows:

''   'DEAR MDLLE. CIBRAS. — I am exerting my utmost influence for you with my father. But he shows no signs of coming round as yet. If I could only induce him to see you! But he is, as you know, a person of unrelenting will, and meanwhile you must confide in my loyal efforts on your behalf. At the same time, I admit that the situation is a precarious one: you are, I am sure, well provided for in the present will of Lord Pharanx, but he is on the point — within, say, three or four days — of making another; and exasperated as he is at your appearance in England, I know there is no chance of your receiving a *centime* under the new will. Before then, however, we must hope that something favorable to you may happen; and in the meantime, let me implore you not to let your only too just resentment pass beyond the bounds of reason.

''   'SINCERELY YOURS,
''   'RANDOLPH.' ''

''I like the letter!'' cried Zaleski. ''You notice the tone of manly candor. But the *facts* — were they true? *Did* the earl make a new will in the time specified?''

"No — but that may have been because his death intervened."

"And in the old will, *was* Mdlle. Cibras provided for?"

"Yes — that at least was correct."

A shadow of pain passed over his face.

"And now," I went on, "I come to the closing scene, in which one of England's foremost men perished by the act of an obscure assassin. The letter I have read was written to Maude Cibras on the fifth of January. The next thing that happens is on the sixth, when Lord Pharanx left his room for another during the whole day, and a skilled mechanic was introduced into it for the purpose of effecting some alterations. Asked by Hester Dyett, as he was leaving the house, what was the nature of his operations, the man replied that he had been applying a patent arrangement to the window looking out on the balcony, for the better protection of the room against burglars, several robberies having recently been committed in the neighborhood. The sudden death of this man, however, before the occurrence of the tragedy, prevented his evidence being heard. On the next day — the seventh — Hester, entering the room with Lord Pharanx's dinner, fancies, though she cannot tell why (inasmuch as his back is towards her, he sitting in an armchair by the fire), that Lord Pharanx has been 'drinking heavily.'

"On the eighth a singular thing befell. The earl was at last induced to see Maude Cibras, and during the morning of that day, with his own hand, wrote a note informing her of his decision, Randolph handing the note to a messenger. The note also has been made public. It reads as follows:

"'MAUDE CIBRAS. — You may come here tonight after dark. Walk to the south side of the house, come up the steps to the balcony, and pass in through the open window to my room. Remember, however, that you have nothing to expect from me, and that from tonight I blot you eternally from my mind: but I will hear your story, which I know beforehand to be false. Destroy this note.

"'Pharanx.'"

As I progressed with my tale, I came to notice that over the countenance of Prince Zaleski there grew little by little a singular fixed aspect. His small, keen features distorted themselves into an expression of what I can only describe as an abnormal *inquisitiveness* — an inquisitiveness most impatient, arrogant, in its intensity. His pupils, contracted each to a dot, became the central *puncta* of two rings of fiery light; his little sharp teeth seemed to gnash. Once before I had seen him look thus greedily, when, grasping a Troglodyte tablet covered with half-effaced hieroglyphics — his fingers livid with the fixity of his grip — he bent on it that strenuous inquisition, that ardent questioning gaze, till, by a species of mesmeric dominancy, he seemed to wrench from it the arcanum it hid from other eyes; then he lay back, pale and faint from the too arduous victory.

When I had read Lord Pharanx's letter, he took the paper eagerly from my hand, and ran his eyes over the passage.

"Tell me — the end," he said.

"Maude Cibras," I went on, "thus invited to a meeting with the earl, failed to make her appearance at the appointed time. It happened that she had left her lodgings in the village early that very morning, and, for some purpose or other, had travelled to the town of Bath. Randolph, too, went away the same day in the opposite direction to Plymouth. He returned on the following morning, the ninth; soon after walked over to Lee; and entered into conversation with the keeper of the inn where Cibras lodged; asked if she was at home, and on being told that she had gone away, asked further if she had taken her luggage with her; was informed that she had, and had also announced her intention of at once leaving England. He then walked away in the direction of the Hall. On this day Hester Dyett noticed that there were many articles of value scattered about the earl's room, notably a tiara of old Brazilian brilliants, sometimes worn by the late Lady Pharanx. Randolph — who was present at the time — further drew her attention to these by telling her that Lord Pharanx had chosen to bring together in his apartment many of the family jewels; and she was instructed to tell the other servants of this fact, in case they should notice any suspicious-looking loafers about the estate.

''On the tenth, both father and son remained in their rooms all day, except when the latter came down to meals; at which times he would lock his door behind him, and with his own hands take in the earl's food, giving as his reason that his father was writing a very important document, and did not wish to be disturbed by the presence of a servant. During the forenoon, Hester Dyett, hearing loud noises in Randolph's room, as if furniture was being removed from place to place, found some pretext for knocking at his door, when he ordered her on no account to interrupt him again, as he was busy packing his clothes in view of a journey to London on the next day. The subsequent conduct of the woman shows that her curiosity must have been excited to the utmost by the undoubtedly strange spectacle of Randolph packing his own clothes. During the afternoon a lad from the village was instructed to collect his companions for a science lecture the same evening at eight o'clock. And so the eventful day wore on.

"We arrive now at this hour of eight P.M. on this tenth day of January. The night is dark and windy; some snow has been falling, but has now ceased. In an upper room is Randolph engaged in expounding the elements of dynamics; in the room under that is Hester Dyett — for Hester has somehow obtained a key that opens the door of Randolph's room, and takes advantage of his absence upstairs to explore it. Under her is Lord Pharanx, certainly in bed, probably asleep. Hester, trembling all over in a fever of fear and excitement, holds a lighted taper in one hand, which she religiously shades with the other; for the storm is gusty, and the gusts, tearing through the crevices of the rattling old casements, toss great flickering shadows on the hangings, which frighten her to death. She has just time to see that the whole room is in the wildest confusion, when suddenly a rougher puff blows out the flame, and she is left in what to her, standing as she was on that forbidden ground, must have been a horror of darkness. At the same moment, clear and sharp from right beneath her, a pistol-shot rings out on her ear. For an instant she stands in stone, incapable of motion. Then on her dazed senses there supervenes — so she swore — the consciousness that some object is moving in the room — moving apparently of its own accord — moving in direct opposition to all the laws of nature as she knows them. She imagines that she perceives a phantasm — a strange something — globular-white — looking, as she says, 'like a good-sized ball of cotton' — rise directly from the floor before her, ascending slowly upward, as if driven aloft by some invisible force. A sharp shock of the sense of the supernatural deprives her of ordered reason. Throwing forward her arms, and uttering a shrill scream, she rushes towards the door. But she never reaches it: midway she falls prostrate over some object, and knows no more; and when, an hour later, she is borne out of the room in the arms of Randolph himself, the blood is dripping from a fracture of her right tibia.

"Meantime, in the upper chamber the pistol-shot and the scream of the woman have been heard. All eyes turn to Randolph. He stands in the shadow of the mechanical contrivance on which he has been illustrating his points; leans for support on it. He essays to speak, the muscles of his face work, but no sound comes. Only after a time is he able to gasp: 'Did you hear something — from below?' They answer 'yes' in chorus; then one of the lads takes a lighted candle, and together they troop out, Randolph behind them. A terrified servant rushes up with the news that something dreadful has happened in the house. They proceed for some distance, but there is an open window on the stairs, and the light is blown out. They have to wait some minutes till another is obtained, and then the procession moves forward once more. Arrived at Lord Pharanx's door, and finding it locked, a lantern is procured, and Randolph leads them through the house and out on the lawn. But having nearly reached the balcony, a lad observes a track of small woman's feet in the snow; a halt is called, and then Randolph points out another track of feet, half obliterated by the snow, extending from a coppice close by up to the balcony, and forming an angle with the first track. These latter are great big feet, made by ponderous laborers' boots. He holds the lantern over the flowerbeds, and shows how they have been trampled down. Some one finds a common scarf, such as workmen wear; and a ring and a

locket, dropped by the burglars in their flight, are also found by
Randolph half-buried in the snow. And now the foremost reach
the window. Randolph, from behind, calls to them to enter.
They cry back that they cannot, the window being closed. At
this reply he seems to be overcome by surprise, by terror. Some
one hears him murmur the words, 'My God, what can have
happened now?' His horror is increased when one of the lads
bears to him a revolting trophy, which has been found just outside the window; it is the front phalanges of three fingers of a
human hand. Again he utters the agonized moan, 'My God!'
and then, mastering his agitation, makes for the window; he
finds that the catch of the sash has been roughly wrenched off, and
that the sash can be opened by merely pushing it up: does so,
and enters. The room is in darkness: on the floor under the window is found the insensible body of the woman Cibras. She is
alive, but has fainted. Her right fingers are closed round the
handle of a large bowie-knife, which is covered with blood; parts
of the left are missing. All the jewelry has been stolen from the
room. Lord Pharanx lies on the bed, stabbed through the bedclothes to the head. Later on a bullet is also found imbedded in
his brain. I should explain that a trenchant edge, running along
the bottom of the sash, was the obvious means by which the
fingers of Cibras had been cut off. This had been placed there a
few days before by the workman I spoke of. Several secret
springs had been placed on the inner side of the lower horizontal
piece of the window-frame, by pressing any one of which the
sash was lowered; so that no one, ignorant of the secret, could
pass out from within, without resting the hand on one of these
springs, and so bringing down the armed sash suddenly on the
underlying hand.

"There was, of course, a trial. The poor culprit, in mortal terror of death, shrieked out a confession of the murder just as the jury had returned from their brief consultation, and before they had time to pronounce their verdict of 'guilty.' But she denied shooting Lord Pharanx, and she denied stealing the jewels; and indeed no pistol and no jewels were found on her, or anywhere in the room. So that many points remain mysterious. What part did the burglars play in the tragedy? Were they in collusion with Cibras? Had the strange behavior of at least one of the inmates of Orven Hall no hidden significance? The wildest guesses were made throughout the country; theories propounded. But no theory explained *all* the points. The ferment, however, has now subsided. Tomorrow morning Maude Cibras ends her life on the gallows.''

Thus I ended my narrative.

Without a word Zaleski rose from the couch, and walked to the organ. Assisted from behind by Ham, who foreknew his master's every whim, he proceeded to render with infinite feeling an air from the *Lakmé* of Delibes; long he sat, dreamily uttering the melody, his head sunken on his breast. When at last he rose, his great expanse of brow was clear, and a smile all but solemn in its serenity was on his lips. He walked up to an ivory *escritoire,* scribbled a few words on a sheet of paper, and handed it to the negro with the order to take my trap and drive with the message in all haste to the nearest telegraph office.

"That message," he said, resuming his place on the couch, "is a last word on the tragedy, and will, no doubt, produce some modification in the final stage of its history. And now, Shiel, let us sit together and confer on this matter. From the manner in which you have expressed yourself, it is evident that there are points which puzzle you — you do not get a clean *coup d'oeil* of the whole regiment of facts, and their causes, and their consequences, as they occurred. Let us see if out of that confusion we cannot produce a coherence, a symmetry. A great wrong is done, and on the society in which it is done is imposed the task of making it translucent, of *seeing* it in all its relations, and of punishing it. But what happens? The society fails to rise to the occasion; on the whole, it contrives to make the opacity more opaque, does not see the crime in any human sense; is unable to punish it. Now this, you will admit, whenever it occurs, is a woeful failure: woeful I mean, not very in itself, but very in its significance: and there must be a precise cause for it. That cause is the lack of something not merely, or specially, in the investigators of the wrong, but in the world at large — shall we not boldly call it the lack of culture? Do not, however, misunderstand me: by the term I mean not so much attainment in general, as *mood* in particular. Whether or when such mood may become universal may be to you a matter of doubt. As for me, I often think that when the era of civilization begins — as assuredly it shall some day begin — when the races of the world cease to be credulous, ovine mobs and become critical, human nations, then will be the ushering in of the ten thousand years of a *clairvoyant* culture. But nowhere, and at no time during the very few hundreds of years that man has occupied the earth, has there been one single sign of its presence. In individuals, yes — in the Greek Plato, and I think in your English Milton and Bishop Berkeley —but in humanity, never; and hardly in any individual outside those two nations. The reason, I fancy, is not so much that man is a hopeless fool, as that Time, so far as he is concerned, has, as we know, only just begun: it being, of course, conceivable that the creation of a perfect society of men, as the first requisite to a *régime* of culture, must nick to itself a longer loop of time than the making of, say, a stratum of coal. A loquacious person — he is one of your cherished 'novel'-writers, by the way, if that be indeed a novel in which there is nowhere any pretence at novelty — once assured me that he could never reflect without swelling on the greatness of the age in which he lived, an age the mighty civilization of which he likened to the Augustan and Periclean. A certain stony gaze of anthropological interest with which I regarded his frontal bone seemed to strike the poor man dumb, and he took a hurried departure. Could he have been ignorant that ours is, in general, greater than the Periclean for the *very* reason that the Divinity is neither the devil nor a bungler; that three thousand years of human consciousness is not nothing; that a whole is greater than its part, and a butterfly than a chrysalis? But it was the assumption that it was therefore in any way great in the abstract that occasioned my profound astonishment, and indeed contempt. Civilization, if it means anything, can only mean the art by which men live musically together — to the lutings, as it were, of Pan-pipes, or say perhaps, to triumphant organ-burst of martial, marching dithyrambs. Any formula defining it as 'the art of lying back and getting elaborately tickled,' should surely at this hour be *too* primitive — *too* Opic — to bring anything but a smile to the lips of grown white-skinned men; and the very fact that such a definition can still find undoubting acceptance in all quarters may be an indication that the true ἰδέα which this condition of being must finally assume is far indeed — far, perhaps, by ages and aeons — from becoming part of the general conception. Nowhere since the beginning has the gross problem of living ever so much as approached solution, much less the delicate and intricate one of living *together: à propos* of which your body-corporate not only still produces criminals (as the body-natural fleas), but its very elementary organism cannot so much as catch a really athletic one as yet. Meanwhile *you* and *I* are handicapped. The individual travaileth in pain. In the struggle for quality, powers, air, he spends his strength, and yet hardly escapes asphyxiation. He can no more wriggle himself free of the psychic gravitations that invest him than the earth can shake herself loose of the sun, or he of the omnipotences that rivet him to the universe. If by chance one shoots a downy hint of wings, an instant feeling of contrast puffs him with self-consciousness: a tragedy at once: the unconscious being 'the alone complete.' To attain to anything, he must needs screw the head up into the atmosphere of the future, while feet and hands drip dark ichors of despair from the crucifying cross of the crude present — *a horrid strain!* Far up a nightly instigation of stars he sees: but he may not strike them with the head. If earth were a boat, and mine, I know well toward what wild azimuths I would compel her helm: but gravity, gravity — chiefest curse of Eden's sin! — is hostile. When indeed (as is ordained), the old mother swings herself into a sublimer orbit, we on her back will follow: till then we make to ourselves Icarian 'organa' in vain. I mean to say that it is the plane of station which is at fault: move that upward, you move all. But meantime is it not Goethe who assures us that 'further reacheth no man, make he what stretching he will'? For Man, you perceive, is not many, but One. It is absurd to suppose that England can be free while Poland is enslaved; Paris is *far* from the beginnings of civilization whilst Toobooloo and Chicago are barbaric. Probably no ill-fated, microcephalous son of Adam

ever tumbled into a mistake quite so huge, so infantile, as did
Dives, if he imagined himself rich while Lazarus sat pauper at
the gate. Not many, I say, but one. Even Ham and I here in our
retreat are not alone; we are embarrassed by the uninvited spirit
of the present; the adamant root of the mountain on whose summit we stand is based ineradicably in the low world. Yet, thank
Heaven, Goethe was not *quite* right — as, indeed, he proved in
his proper person. I tell you, Shiel, I *know* whether Mary did or
did not murder Darnley; I know — as clearly, as precisely, as a
man can know — that Beatrice Cenci was not 'guilty' as certain
recently-discovered documents 'prove' her, but that the Shelley
version of the affair, though a guess, is the correct one. It *is*
possible, by taking thought, to add one cubit — or say a hand,
or a dactyl — to your stature; you *may* develop powers slightly
— very slightly, but distinctly, both in kind and degree — in advance of those of the mass who live in or about the same cycle of
time in which you live. But it is only when the powers to which
I refer are shared by the mass — when what, for want of another
term, I call the age of the Cultured Mood has at length arrived
—that their exercise will become easy and familiar to the individual; and who shall say what presciences, prisms, *séances,*
what introspective craft, Genie apocalypses, shall not *then*
become possible to the few who stand spiritually in the van of
men.

"All this, you will understand, I say as some sort of excuse
for myself, and for you, for any hesitation we may have shown
in loosening the very little puzzle you have placed before me —
one which we certainly must not regard as difficult of solution.
Of course, looking at all the facts, the first consideration that
must inevitably rivet the attention is that arising from the cir-

cumstance that Viscount Randolph has strong reasons to wish his father dead. They are avowed enemies; he is the *fiancé* of a princess whose husband he is probably too poor to become, though he will very likely be rich enough when his father dies; and so on. All that appears on the surface. On the other hand, we — you and I — know the man: he is a person of gentle blood, as moral, we suppose, as ordinary people, occupying a high station in the world. It is impossible to imagine that such a person would commit an assassination, or even countenance one, for any or all of the reasons that present themselves. In our hearts, with or without clear proof, we could hardly believe it of him. Earls' sons do not, in fact, go about murdering people. Unless, then, we can so reason as to discover other motives — strong, adequate, irresistible — and by 'irresistible' I mean a motive which must be *far* stronger than even the love of life itself — we should, I think, in fairness dismiss him from our mind.

"And yet it must be admitted that his conduct is not free of blame. He contracts a sudden intimacy with the acknowledged culprit, whom he does not seem to have known before. He meets her by night, corresponds with her. Who and what is this woman? I think we could not be far wrong in guessing some very old flame of Lord Pharanx's of *Théâtre des Variétés* type, whom he has supported for years, and from whom, hearing some story to her discredit, he threatens to withdraw his supplies. However that be, Randolph writes to Cibras — a violent woman, a woman of lawless passions — assuring her that in four or five days she will be excluded from the will of his father; and in four or five days Cibras plunges a knife into his father's bosom. It is a perfectly natural sequence — though, of course, the *intention* to produce by his words the actual effect produced might have been absent; indeed, the letter of Lord Pharanx himself, had it been received, would have tended to produce that very effect; for it not only gives an excellent opportunity for converting into action those evil thoughts which Randolph (thoughtlessly or guiltily) has instilled, but it further tends to rouse her passions by cutting off from her all hopes of favor. If we presume, then, as is only natural, that there was no such intention on the part of the earl, we *may* make the same presumption in the case of the son. Cibras, however, never receives the earl's letter: on the morning of the same day she goes to Bath, with the double object, I suppose, of purchasing a weapon, and creating an impression that she has left the country. How then does she know the exact *locale* of Lord Pharanx's room? It is in an unusual part of the mansion, she is unacquainted with any of the servants, a stranger to the district. Can it be possible that Randolph *had told her?* And here again, even in that case, you must bear in mind that Lord Pharanx also told her in his note, and you must recognize the possibility of the absence of evil intention on the part of the son. Indeed, I may go further and show you that in all but every instance in which his actions are in themselves *outré,* suspicious, they are rendered, not less *outré,* but less suspicious, by the fact that Lord Pharanx himself knew of them, shared in them. There was the cruel barbing of that balcony window; about it the crudest thinker would argue thus to himself: 'Randolph practically incites Maude Cibras to murder his father on the fifth, and on the sixth he has that window so altered in order that, should she act on his suggestion, she will be caught on attempting to leave the room, while he himself, the actual culprit being discovered *en flagrant délit,* will escape every shadow of suspicion.' But, on the other hand, we know that the alteration was made with Lord Pharanx's consent, most likely on his initiative — for he leaves his favored room during a whole day for that very purpose. So with the letter to Cibras on the eighth — Randolph despatches it, but the earl writes it. So with the disposal of the jewels in the apartment on the ninth. There had been some burglaries in the neighborhood, and the suspicion at once arises in the mind of the crude reasoner: Could Randolph — finding now that Cibras has 'left the country,' that, in fact, the tool he had expected to serve his ends has failed him — could he have thus brought those jewels there, and thus warned the servants of their presence, in the hope that the intelligence might so get abroad and lead to a burglary, in the course of which his father might lose his life? There are evidences, you know, tending to show that the burglary did actually at last take place, and the suspicion is, in view of that, by no means unreasonable. And yet, militating against it, is our knowledge that it was Lord Pharanx who *'chose'* to gather the jewels round him; that it was in his presence that Randolph drew the attention of the servant to them. In the matter, at least, of the little political comedy the son seems to have acted alone; but you surely cannot rid yourself of the impression that the radical speeches, the candidature, and the rest of it, formed all of them only a very elaborate, and withal clumsy, set of preliminaries to the *class.* Anything, to make the perspective, the sequence of *that* seem natural. But in the class, at any rate, we have the tacit acquiescence, or even the cooperation, of Lord Pharanx. You have described the conspiracy of quiet which, for some reason or other, was imposed on the household; in that reign of silence the bang of a door, the fall of a plate, becomes a domestic tornado. But have you ever heard an agricultural laborer in clogs or heavy boots ascend a stair? The noise is terrible. The tramp of an army of them through the house and overhead, probably jabbering uncouthly together, would be insufferable. Yet Lord Pharanx seems to have made no objection; the novel institution is set up in his own mansion, in an unusual part of it, probably against his own principles; but we hear of no murmur from him. On the fatal day, too, the calm of the house is rudely broken by a considerable commotion in Randolph's room just overhead, caused by his preparation for 'a journey to London.' But the usual angry remonstrance is not forthcoming from the master. And do you not see how all this more than acquiescence of Lord Pharanx in the conduct of his son deprives that conduct of half its significance, its intrinsic suspiciousness?

"A hasty reasoner then would inevitably jump to the conclusion that Randolph was guilty of something — some evil intention — though of precisely what he would remain in doubt. But a more careful reasoner would pause: he would reflect that *as* the father was implicated in those acts, and *as* he was innocent of any such intention, so might possibly, even probably, be the son. This, I take it, has been the view of the officials, whose logic is probably far in advance of their imagination. But supposing we can adduce one act, undoubtedly actuated by evil intention on the part of Randolph — one act in which his father certainly did *not* participate — what follows next? Why, that we revert at once to the view of the hasty reasoner, and conclude that *all* the other acts in the same relation were actuated by the same evil motive; and having reached that point, we shall be unable longer to resist the conclusion that those of them in which his father had a share *might* have sprung from a like motive in *his* mind also; nor should the mere obvious impossibility of such a condition of things have even the very least influence on us, as thinkers, in causing us to close our minds against its logical possibility. I therefore make the inference, and pass on.

"Let us then see if we can by searching find out any absolutely certain deviation from right on the part of Randolph, in which we may be quite sure that his father was not an abettor. At eight on the night of the murder it is dark; there has been some snow, but the fall has ceased — how long before I know not, but so long that the interval becomes sufficiently appreciable to cause remark. Now the party going round the house come on two tracks of feet meeting at an angle. Of one track we are merely told that it was made by the small foot of a woman, and of it we know no more; of the other we learn that the feet were big and the boots clumsy, and, it is added the marks were *half obliterated by the snow.* Two things then are clear: that the persons who made them came from different directions, and probably made them at different times. That, alone, by the way, may be a sufficient answer to your question as to whether Cibras was in collusion with the 'burglars.' But how does Randolph behave with reference to these tracks? Though he carries the lantern, he fails to perceive the first — the woman's — the discovery of which is made by a lad; but the second, half-hidden in the snow, he notices readily enough, and at once points it out. He explains that burglars have been on the warpath. But examine his horror of surprise when he hears that the window is closed; when he sees the woman's bleeding fingers. He cannot help exclaiming, 'My God! what has happened *now?*' But why 'now'? The word cannot refer to his father's death, for that he knew, or guessed, beforehand, having heard the shot. Is it not rather the exclamation of a man whose schemes destiny has complicated? Besides, he should have *expected* to find the window closed: no one except himself, Lord Pharanx, and the workman, who was now dead, knew the secret of its construction; the burglars therefore, having entered and robbed the room, one of them, intending to go out, would press on the ledge, and the sash would fall on his hand with what result we know. The others would then either break the glass and so escape; or pass through the house; or remain prisoners. That immoderate surprise was therefore absurdly illogical, after seeing the burglar-track in the snow. But how, above all, do you account for Lord Pharanx's silence during and after the burglars' visit — if there was a visit? He was, you must remember, alive all that time; *they* did not kill him; certainly they did not shoot him, for the shot is heard after the snow has ceased to fall — that is, after, long after, they have left, since it was the falling snow that had half obliterated their tracks; nor did they stab him, for to this Cibras confesses. Why then, being alive, and not gagged, did he give no token of the presence of his visitors? There were in fact no burglars at Orven Hall that night."

"But the track!" I cried, "the jewels found in the snow — the neckerchief!"

Zaleski smiled.

"Burglars," he said, "are plain, honest folk who have a just notion of the value of jewelry when they see it. They very properly regard it as mere foolish waste to drop precious stones about in the snow, and would refuse to company with a man weak enough to let fall his neckerchief on a cold night. The whole business of the burglars was a particularly inartistic trick, unworthy of its author. The mere facility with which Randolph discovered the buried jewels by the aid of a dim lantern, should have served as a hint to an educated police not afraid of facing the improbable. The jewels had been *put* there with the object of throwing suspicion on the imaginary burglars; with the same design the catch of the window had been wrenched off, the sash purposely left open, the track made, the valuables taken from Lord Pharanx's room. All this was deliberately done by someone — would it be rash to say at once by whom?

"Our suspicions having now lost their whole character of vagueness, and begun to lead us in a perfectly definite direction, let us examine the statements of Hester Dyett. Now, it is immediately comprehensible to me that the evidence of this woman at the public examinations was looked at askance. There can be no doubt that she is a poor specimen of humanity, an undesirable servant, a peering, hysterical caricature of a woman. Her statements, if formally recorded, were not believed; or if believed, were believed with only half the mind. No attempt was made to deduce anything from them. But for my part, if I wanted specially reliable evidence as to any matter of fact, it is precisely from such a being that I would seek it. Let me draw you a picture of that class of intellect. They have a greed for information, but the information, to satisfy them, must relate to actualities; they have no sympathy with fiction; it is from their impatience of what seems to be that springs their curiosity of what *is*. Clio is their muse, and she alone. Their whole lust is to gather knowledge through a hole, their whole faculty is to *peep*. But they are destitute of imagination, and do not lie; in their passion for realities they would esteem it a sacrilege to distort history. They make straight for the substantial, the indubitable.

For this reason the Peniculi and Ergasili of Plautus seem to me far more true to nature than the character of Paul Pry in Jerrold's comedy. In one instance, indeed, the evidence of Hester Dyett appears, on the surface of it, to be quite false. She declares that she sees a round white object moving upward in the room. But the night being gloomy, her taper having gone out, she must have been standing in a dense darkness. How then could she see this object? Her evidence, it was argued, must be designedly false, or else (as she was in an ecstatic condition) the result of an excited fancy. But I have stated that such persons, nervous, neurotic even as they may be, are not fanciful. I therefore accept her evidence as true. And now, mark the consequence of that acceptance. I am driven to admit that there must, from some source, have been light in the room — a light faint enough, and diffused enough, to escape the notice of Hester herself. This being so, it must have proceeded from around, from below, or from above. There are no other alternatives. Around these was nothing but the darkness of the night; the room beneath, we know, was also in darkness. The light then came from the room above — from the mechanic classroom. But there is only one possible means by which the light from an upper can diffuse a lower room. It *must* be by a hole in the intermediate boards. We are thus driven to the discovery of an aperture of some sort in the flooring of that upper chamber. Given this, the mystery of the round white object 'driven' upward disappears. We at once ask, why not *drawn* upward through the newly-discovered aperture by a string too small to be visible in the gloom? Assuredly it was drawn upward. And now having established a hole in the ceiling of the room in which Hester stands, is it unreasonable — even without further evidence — to suspect another in the flooring? But we actually have this further evidence. As she rushes to the door she falls, faints, and fractures the lower part of her leg. Had she fallen *over* some object, as you supposed, the result might have been a fracture also, but in a different part of the body; being where it was, it could only have been caused by placing the foot inadvertently in a hole while the rest of the body was in rapid motion. But this gives us an approximate idea of the *size* of the lower hole; it was at least big enough to admit the foot and lower leg, big enough therefore to admit that 'good-sized ball of cotton' of which the woman speaks: and from the lower we are able to conjecture the size of the upper. But how comes it that these holes are nowhere mentioned in the evidence? It can only be because no one ever saw them. Yet the rooms must have been examined by the police, who, if they existed, must have seen them. They therefore did not exist: that is to say, the pieces which had been removed from the floorings had by that time been neatly replaced, and, in the case of the lower one, covered by the carpet, the removal of which had caused so much commotion in Randolph's room on the fatal day. Hester Dyett would have been able to notice and bring at least one of the apertures forward in evidence, but she fainted before she had time to find out the cause of her fall, and an hour later it was, you remember, Randolph himself who bore her from the room. But should not the aperture in the top floor have been observed by the class? Undoubtedly, if its position was in the open space in the middle of the room. But it was not observed, and therefore its position was not there, but in the only other place left — behind the apparatus used in demonstration. That then was *one* useful object which the apparatus — and with it the elaborate hypocrisy of class, and speeches, and candidature — served: it was made to act as a curtain, a screen. But had it no other purpose? That question we may answer when we know its name and its nature. And it is not beyond our powers to conjecture this with something like certainty. For the only 'machines' possible to use in illustration of simple mechanics are the screw, the wedge, the scale, the lever, the wheel-and-axle, and At-wood's machine. The mathematical principles which any of these exemplify would, of course, be incomprehensible to such a class, but the first five most of all, and as there would naturally be some slight pretence of trying to make the learners understand, I therefore select the last; and this selection is justified when we remember that on the shot being heard, Randolph leans for support on the 'machine,' and stands in its shadow; but any of the others would be too small to throw any appreciable shadow, except one — the wheel-and-axle — and that one would hardly afford support to a tall man in the erect position. The Atwood's machine is therefore forced on us; as to its construction, it is, as you are aware, composed of two upright posts, with a cross-bar fitted with pulleys and strings, and is intended to show the motion of bodies acting under a constant force — the force of gravity, to wit. But now consider all the really glorious uses to which those same pulleys may be turned in lowering and lifting unobserved that 'ball of cotton' through the two apertures, while the other strings with the weights attached are dangling before the dull eyes of the peasants. I need only point out that when the whole company trooped out of the room, Randolph was the last to leave it, and it is not now difficult to conjecture why.

"Of what, then, have we convicted Randolph? For one thing,

we have shown that by marks of feet in the snow preparation was made beforehand for obscuring the cause of the earl's death. That death must therefore have been at least expected, foreknown. Thus we convict him of expecting it. And then, by an independent line of deduction, we can also discover the *means* by which he expected it to occur. It is clear that he did not expect it to occur when it did by the hand of Maude Cibras — for this is proved by his knowledge that she had left the neighborhood, by his evidently genuine astonishment at the sight of the closed window, and, above all, by his truly morbid desire to establish a substantial, an irrefutable *alibi* for himself by going to Plymouth on the day when there was every reason to suppose she would do the deed — that is, on the eighth, the day of the earl's invitation. On the fatal night, indeed, the same morbid eagerness to build up a clear *alibi* is observable, for he surrounds himself with a cloud of witnesses in the upper chamber. But that, you will admit, is not nearly so perfect a one as a journey, say, to Plymouth would have been. Why then, expecting the death, did he not take some such journey? Obviously because on *this* occasion his personal presence was necessary. When, *in conjunction* with this, we recall the fact that during the intrigues with Cibras the lectures were discontinued, and again resumed immediately on her unlooked-for departure, we arrive at the conclusion that the means by which Lord Pharanx's death was expected to occur was the personal presence of Randolph *in conjunction* with the political speeches, the candidature, the class, the apparatus.

"But though he stands condemned of foreknowing, and being in some sort connected with, his father's death, I can nowhere find any indication of his having personally accomplished it, or even of his ever having had any such intention. The evidence is evidence of complicity — and nothing more. And yet — and yet — even of *this* we began by acquitting him unless we could discover, as I said, some strong, adequate, altogether irresistible motive for such complicity. Failing this, we ought to admit that at some point our argument has played us false, and led us into conclusions wholly at variance with our certain knowledge of the principles underlying human conduct in general. Let us therefore seek for such a motive — something deeper than personal enmity, stronger than personal ambition, *than the love of life itself!* And now, tell me, at the time of the occurrence of this mystery, was the whole past history of the House of Orven fully investigated?"

"Not to my knowledge," I answered; "in the papers there were, of course, sketches of the earl's career, but that I think was all."

"Yet it cannot be that their past was unknown, but only that it was ignored. Long, I tell you, long and often, have I pondered on that history, and sought to trace with what ghastly secret has been pregnant the destiny, gloomful as Erebus and the murk of black-peplosed Nux, which for centuries has hung its pall over the men of this ill-fated house. Now at last I know. Dark, dark, and red with gore and horror is that history; down the silent corridors of the ages have these blood-soaked sons of Atreus fled shrieking before the pursuing talons of the dread Eumenides. The first earl received his patent in 1535 from the eighth Henry. Two years later, though noted as a rabid 'king's man,' he joined the Pilgrimage of Grace against his master, and was soon after executed, with Darcy and some other lords. His age was then fifty. His son, meantime, had served in the king's army under Norfolk. It is remarkable, by the way, that females have all along been rare in the family, and that in no instance has there been more than one son. The second earl, under the sixth Edward, suddenly threw up a civil post, hastened to the army, and fell at the age of forty at the battle of Pinkie in 1547. He was accompanied by his son. The third in 1557, under Mary, renounced the Catholic faith, to which, both before and since, the family have passionately clung, and suffered (at the age of forty) the last penalty. The fourth earl died naturally, but suddenly, in his bed at the age of fifty during the winter of 1566. At midnight *of the same day* he was laid in the grave by his son. This son was later on, in 1591, seen by *his* son to fall from a lofty balcony at Orven Hall, while walking in his sleep at high noonday. Then for some time nothing happens; but the eighth earl dies mysteriously in 1651 at the age of forty-five. A fire occurring in his room, he leapt from a window to escape the flames. Some of his limbs were thereby fractured, but he was in a fair way to recovery when there was a sudden relapse, soon ending in death. He was found to have been poisoned by *radix aconiti indica,* a rare Arabian poison not known in Europe at that time except to *savants,* and first mentioned by Acosta some months before. An attendant was accused and tried, but acquitted. The then son of the House was a Fellow of the newly-founded Royal Society, and author of a now-forgotten work on Toxicology, which, however, I have read. No suspicion, of course, fell on *him.*''

As Zaleski proceeded with his retrospect, I could not but ask myself with stirrings of the most genuine wonder, whether he could possess this intimate knowledge of *all* the great families of

Europe! It was as if he had spent a part of his life in making special study of the history of the Orvens.

"In the same manner," he went on, "I could detail the annals of the family from that time to the present. But all through they have been marked by the same latent tragic elements; and I have said enough to show you that in each of the tragedies there was invariably something large, leering, something of which the mind demands explanation, but seeks in vain to find it. Now we need no longer seek. Destiny did not design that the last Lord of Orven should any more hide from the world the guilty secret of his race. It was the will of the gods — and he betrayed himself. 'Return,' he writes, 'the beginning of the end is come.' What end? *The* end — perfectly well known to Randolph, needing no explanation for *him*. The old, old end, which in the ancient dim time led the first lord, loyal still at heart, to forsake his king; and another, still devout, to renounce his cherished faith, and yet another to set fire to the home of his ancestors. You have called the two last scions of the family 'a proud and selfish pair of beings'; proud they were, and selfish too, but you are in error if you think their selfishness a personal one: on the contrary, they were singularly oblivious of self in the ordinary sense of the word. Theirs was the pride and the selfishness of *race*. What consideration, think you, other than the weal of his house, could induce Lord Randolph to take on himself the shame — for as such he certainly regards it — of a conversion to radicalism? He would, I am convinced, have *died* rather than make his pretence for merely personal ends. But he does it — and the reason? It is because he has received that awful summons from home; because 'the end' is daily coming nearer, and it must not find him unprepared to meet it; it is because Lord Pharanx's senses are becoming *too* acute; because the clatter of the servants' knives at the other end of the house inflames him to madness; because his excited palate can no longer endure any food but the subtlest delicacies; because Hester Dyett is able from the posture in which he sits to conjecture that he is intoxicated; because, in fact, he is on the brink of the dreadful malady which physicians call *'General Paralysis of the Insane.'* You remember I took from your hands the newspaper containing the earl's letter to Cibras, in order to read it with my own eyes. I had my reasons, and I was justified. That letter contains three mistakes in spelling: 'here' is printed 'hear,' 'pass' appears as 'pas,' and 'room' as 'rume.' Printers' errors, you say? But not so — one might be, two in that short paragraph could hardly be, three would be impossible. Search the whole paper through, and I think you will not find another. Let us reverence the theory of probabilities: the errors were the writer's, not the printer's. General paralysis of the insane is known to have this effect on the writing. It attacks its victims about the period of middle age — the age at which the deaths of all the Orvens who died mysteriously occurred. Finding then that the dire heritage of his race — the heritage of madness — is falling or fallen on him, he summons his son from India. On himself he passes sentence of death: it is the tradition of the family, the secret vow of self-destruction handed down through ages from father to son. But he must have aid: in these days it is difficult for a man to commit the suicidal act without detection — and if madness is a disgrace to the race, equally so is suicide. Besides, the family is to be enriched by the insurances on his life, and is thereby to be allied with royal blood; but the money will be lost if the suicide be detected. Randolph therefore returns and blossoms into a popular candidate.

"For a time he is led to abandon his original plans by the appearance of Maude Cibras; he hopes that *she* may be made to destroy the earl; but when she fails him, he recurs to it — recurs to it all suddenly, for Lord Pharanx's condition is rapidly becoming critical, patent to all eyes, could any eye see him — so much so that on the last day none of the servants are allowed to enter his room. We must therefore regard Cibras as a mere addendum to, an extraneous element in, the tragedy, not as an integral part of it. She did not shoot the noble lord, for she had no pistol; nor did Randolph, for he was at a distance from the bed of death, surrounded by witnesses; nor did the imaginary burglars. The earl therefore shot himself; and it was the small globular silver pistol, such as this" — here Zaleski drew a little embossed Venetian weapon from a drawer near him — "that appeared in the gloom to the excited Hester as a 'ball of cotton,' while it was being drawn upward by the Atwood's machine. But if the earl shot himself he could not have done so *after* being stabbed to the heart. Maude Cibras, therefore, stabbed a dead man. She would, of course, have ample time for stealing into the room and doing so after the shot was fired, and before the party reached the balcony window, on account of the delay on the stairs in procuring a second light; in going to the earl's door; in examining the tracks, and so on. But having stabbed a dead man, she is not guilty of murder. The message I just now sent by Ham was one addressed to the Home Secretary, telling him on no account to let Cibras die tomorrow. He well knows my name, and will hardly be silly enough to suppose me capable of using words without meaning. It will be perfectly easy to prove my conclusions, for the pieces removed from, and replaced in, the floorings can still be detected, if looked for; the pistol is still, no doubt, in Randolph's room, and its bore can be compared with the bullet found in Lord Pharanx's brain; above all, the jewels stolen by the 'burglars' are still safe in some cabinet of the new earl, and may readily be discovered. I therefore expect that the *dénoûment* will now take a somewhat different turn.''

That the *dénoûment* did take a different turn, and pretty strictly in accordance with Zaleski's forecast, is now matter of history, and the incidents, therefore, need no further comment from me in this place.

The Stone of the
Edmundsbury Monks

"Russia," said Prince Zaleski to me one day, when I happened to be on a visit to him in his darksome sanctuary — "Russia may be regarded as land surrounded by ocean; that is to say, she is an island. In the same way, it is sheer gross irrelevancy to speak of *Britain* as an island, unless indeed the word be understood as a mere *modus loquendi* arising out of a rather poor geographical pleasantry. Britain, in reality, is a small continent. Near her — a little to the southeast — is situated the large island of Europe. Thus, the enlightened French traveller passing to these shores should commune within himself: 'I now cross to the Mainland'; and retracing his steps: 'I now return to the fragment rent by wrack and earthshock from the Mother-country.' And this I say not in the way of paradox, but as the expression of a sober truth. I have in my mind merely the relative depth and extent — the *non-insularity,* in fact — of the impressions made by the several nations of the world. But this island of Europe has herself an island of her own: the name of it, Russia. She, of all lands, is the *terra incognita,* the unknown land; till quite lately she was more — she was the undiscovered, the unsuspected land. She *has* a literature, you know, and a history, and a language, and a purpose — but of all this the world has hardly so much as heard. Indeed, she, and not any Antarctic Sea whatever, is the real Ultima Thule of modern times, the true Island of Mystery."

I reproduce these remarks of Zaleski here, not so much on account of the splendid tribute to my country contained in them, as because it ever seemed to me — and especially in connection with the incident I am about to recall — that in this respect at least he was a genuine son of Russia; if she is the Land, so truly was he the Man, of Mystery. I who knew him best alone knew that it was impossible to know him. He was a being little of the present: with one arm he embraced the whole past; the fingers of the other heaved on the vibrant pulse of the future. He seemed to me — I say it deliberately and with forethought — to possess the unparalleled power not merely of disentangling in retrospect, but of unravelling in prospect, and I have known him to relate *coming* events with unimaginable minuteness of precision. He was nothing if not superlative: his diatribes, now culminating in a very *extravaganza* of hyperbole — now sailing with loose wing through the downy, witched, Dutch cloud-heaps of some quaintest tramontane Nephelococcugia of thought — now laying down law of the Medes for the actual world of today — had oft-times the strange effect of bringing back to my mind the very singular old-epic epithet, ἠνεμόεν — *airy* — as applied to human thought. The mere grip of his memory was not simply extraordinary, it had in it a token, a hint, of the strange, the pythic — nay, the sibylline. And as his reflecting intellect, moreover, had all the lightness of foot of a chamois kid, unless you could contrive to follow each dazzling swift successive step, by the sum of which he attained his Alp-heights, he inevitably left on you the astounding, the confounding impression of mental omnipresence.

I had brought with me a certain document, a massive book

bound in iron and leather, the diary of one Sir Jocelin Saul. This I had abstracted from a gentleman of my acquaintance, the head of a firm of inquiry agents in London, into whose hand, only the day before, it had come. A distant neighbor of Sir Jocelin, hearing by chance of his extremity, had invoked the assistance of this firm; but the aged baronet, being in a state of the utmost feebleness, terror, and indeed hysterical incoherence, had been able to utter no word in explanation of his condition or wishes, and, in silent abandonment, had merely handed the book to the agent.

A day or two after I had reached the desolate old mansion which the prince occupied, knowing that he might sometimes be induced to take an absorbing interest in questions that had proved themselves too profound, or too intricate, for ordinary solution, I asked him if he was willing to hear the details read out from the diary, and on his assenting, I proceeded to do so.

The brief narrative had reference to a very large and very valuable oval gem enclosed in the substance of a golden chalice, which chalice, in the monastery of St. Edmundsbury, had once lain centuries long within the Loculus, or inmost coffin, wherein reposed the body of St. Edmund. By pressing a hidden pivot, the cup (which was composed of two equal parts, connected by minute hinges) sprang open, and in a hollow space at the bottom was disclosed the gem. Sir Jocelin Saul, I may say, was lineally connected with — though, of course, not descendant from — that same Jocelin of Brakelonda, a brother of the Edmundsbury convent, who wrote the now so celebrated *Jocelini Chronica:* and the chalice had fallen into the possession of the family, seemingly at some time prior to the suppression of the monastery about 1537. On it was inscribed in old English characters of unknown date the words:

> "Shulde this Ston stalen bee,
>   Or shuld it chaunges dre,
>   The Houss of Sawl and hys Hed anoon shal de."

The stone itself was an intaglio, and had engraved on its surface the figure of a mythological animal, together with some nearly obliterated letters, of which the only ones remaining legible were those forming the word "Has." As a sure precaution against the loss of the gem, another cup had been made and engraved in an exactly similar manner, inside of which, to complete the delusion, another stone of the same size and cut, but of comparatively valueless material, had been placed.

Sir Jocelin Saul, a man of intense nervosity, lived his life alone in a remote old manor-house in Suffolk, his only companion being a person of Eastern origin, named Ul-Jabal. The baronet had consumed his vitality in the life-long attempt to sound the too fervid Maelstrom of Oriental research, and his mind had perhaps caught from his studies a tinge of their morbidness, their esotericism, their insanity. He had for some years past been engaged in the task of writing a stupendous work on Pre-Zoroastrian Theogonies, in which, it is to be supposed, Ul-Jabal acted somewhat in the capacity of secretary. But I will give *verbatim* the extracts from his diary:

"*June 11.* This is my birthday. Seventy years ago exactly I slid from the belly of the great Dark into this Light and Life. My

God! My God! it is briefer than the rage of an hour, fleeter than a mid-day trance. Ul-Jabal greeted me warmly — seemed to have been looking forward to it — and pointed out that seventy is of the fateful numbers, its only factors being seven, five, and two: the last denoting the duality of Birth and Death; five, Isolation; seven, Infinity. I informed him that this was also my father's birthday; and *his* father's; and repeated the oft-told tale of how the latter, just seventy years ago today, walking at twilight by the churchyard-wall, saw the figure of *himself* sitting on a gravestone, and died five weeks later riving with the pangs of hell. Whereat the sceptic showed his two huge rows of teeth.

''What is his peculiar interest in the Edmundsbury chalice? On each successive birthday when the cup has been produced, he has asked me to show him the stone. Without any well-defined reason I have always declined, but today I yielded. He gazed long into its sky-blue depth, and then asked if I had no idea what the inscription 'Has' meant. I informed him that it was one of the lost secrets of the world.

''*June 15.*— Some new element has entered into our existence here. Something threatens me. I hear the echo of a menace against my sanity and my life. It is as if the garment which enwraps me has grown too hot, too heavy for me. A notable drowsiness has settled on my brain — a drowsiness in which thought, though slow, is a thousandfold more fiery-vivid than ever. Oh, fair goddess of Reason, desert not me, thy chosen child!

''*June 18.* — Ul-Jabal? — that man is *the very Devil incarnate!*

''*June 19.* — So much for my bounty, all my munificence, to this poisonous worm. I picked him up on the heights of the

Mountain of Lebanon, a cultured savage among cultured savages, and brought him here to be a prince of thought by my side. What though his plundered wealth — the debt I owe him — has saved me from a sort of ruin? Have not *I* instructed him in the sweet secret of Reason?

"I lay back on my bed in the lonely morning watches, my soul heavy as with the distilled essence of opiates, and in vivid vision knew that he had entered my apartment. In the twilight gloom his glittering rows of shark's teeth seemed impacted on my eyeball — I saw *them,* and nothing else. I was not aware when he vanished from the room. But at daybreak I crawled on hands and knees to the cabinet containing the chalice. The viperous murderer! He has stolen my gem, well knowing that with it he has stolen my life. The stone is gone — gone, my precious gem. A weakness overtook me, and I lay for many dreamless hours naked on the marble floor.

"Does the fool think to hide ought from my eyes? Can he imagine that I shall not recover my precious gem, my stone of Saul?

"*June 20.* — Ah, Ul-Jabal — my brave, my noble Son of the Prophet of God! He has replaced the stone! He would not slay an aged man. The yellow ray of his eye, it is but the gleam of the great thinker, not — not — the gleam of the assassin. Again, as I lay in semi-somnolence, I saw him enter my room, this time more distinctly. He went up to the cabinet. Shaking the chalice in the dawning, some hours after he had left, I heard with delight the rattle of the stone. I might have known he would replace it; I should not have doubted his clemency to a poor man like me. But the strange being! — he has taken the *other* stone from the *other* cup — a thing of little value to any man! Is Ul-Jabal mad or I?

"*June 21.* — Merciful Lord in Heaven! he has *not* replaced it — not *it* —but another instead of it. Today I actually opened the chalice, and saw. He has put a stone there, the same in size, in cut, in engraving, but different in color, in quality, in value — a stone I have never seen before. How has he obtained it — whence? I must brace myself to probe, to watch; I must turn myself into an eye to search this devil's-bosom. My life, this subtle, cunning reason of mine, hangs in the balance.

"*June 22.* — Just now he offered me a cup of wine. I almost dashed it to the ground before him. But he looked steadfastly into my eye. I flinched: and drank — drank.

"Years ago, when, as I remember, we were at Balbec, I saw him one day make an almost tasteless preparation out of pure black nicotine, which in mere wanton lust he afterwards gave to some of the dwellers by the Caspian to drink. But the fiend would surely never dream of giving to me that browse of hell — to me an aged man, and a thinker, a seer.

"*June 23.* — The mysterious, the unfathomable Ul-Jabal! Once again, as I lay in heavy trance at midnight, has he invaded, calm and noiseless as a spirit, the sanctity of my chamber. Serene on the swaying air, which, radiant with soft beams of vermil and violet light, rocked me into variant visions of heaven, I reclined and regarded him unmoved. The man has replaced the valueless stone in the modern-made chalice, and has now stolen the false stone from the other, which *he himself* put there! In patience will I possess this my soul, and watch what shall betide. My eyes shall know no slumber!

"*June 24.* — No more — no more shall I drink wine from the hand of Ul-Jabal. My knees totter beneath the weight of my lean body. Daggers of lambent fever race through my brain incessant. Some fibrillary twitchings at the right angle of the mouth have also arrested my attention.

"*June 25.* — He has dared at open mid-day to enter my room. I watched him from an angle of the stairs pass along the corridor and open my door. But for the terrifying, death-boding thump, thump of my heart, I should have faced the traitor then, and told him that I knew all his treachery. Did I say that I had strange fibrillary twitchings at the right angle of my mouth, and a brain on fire? I have ceased to write my book — the more pity for the world, not for me.

"*June 26.* — Marvellous to tell, the traitor, Ul-Jabal, has now placed *another* stone in the Edmundsbury chalice — also identical in nearly every respect with the original gem. This, then, was the object of his entry into my room yesterday. So that he has first stolen the real stone and replaced it by another; then he has stolen this other and replaced it by yet another; he has beside stolen the valueless stone from the modern chalice, and then replaced it. Surely a man gone rabid, a man gone dancing, foaming, raving mad!

"*June 28.* — I have now set myself to the task of recovering my jewel. It is here, and I shall find it. Life against life — and which is the best life, mine or this accursed Ishmaelite's? If need be, I will do murder — I, with this withered hand — so that I get back the heritage which is mine.

"Today, when I thought he was wandering in the park, I stole into his room, locking the door on the inside. I trembled exceedingly, knowing that his eyes are in every place. I ransacked the chamber, dived among his clothes, but found no stone. One singular thing in a drawer I saw: a long, white beard, and a wig of long and snow-white hair. As I passed out of the chamber, lo, he stood face to face with me at the door in the passage. My heart gave one bound, and then seemed wholly to cease its travail. Oh, I must be sick unto death, weaker than a bruised reed! When I woke from my swoon he was supporting me in his arms. 'Now,' he said, grinning down at me, 'now you have at last delivered all into my hands.' He left me, and I saw him go into his room and lock the door upon himself. What is it I have delivered into the madman's hands?

"*July 1.* — Life against life — and his, the young, the stalwart, rather than mine, the mouldering, the sere. I love life. Not *yet* am I ready to weigh anchor, and reeve halliard, and turn my prow over the watery paths of the wine-brown deeps. Oh no. Not yet. Let *him* die. Many and many are the days in which I shall yet see the light, walk, think. I am averse to end the number of my years: there is even a feeling in me at times that this worn body shall never, never taste of death. The chalice predicts indeed that I and my house shall end when the stone is lost — a mere fiction *at first,* an idler's dream *then,* but now — now — that the prophecy has stood so long a part of the reality of things, and a fact among facts — no longer fiction, but Adamant, stern as the very word of God. Do I not feel hourly since it has gone how the surges of life ebb, ebb ever lower in my heart? Nay, nay, but there is hope. I have here beside me an Arab blade of subtle Damascene steel, insinuous to pierce and to hew, with which in a street of Bethlehem I saw a Syrian's head cleft open — a gallant stroke! The edges of this I have made bright and white for a nuptial of blood.

"*July 2.* — I spent the whole of the last night in searching every nook and crack of the house, using a powerful magnifying lens. At times I thought Ul-Jabal was watching me, and would pounce out and murder me. Convulsive tremors shook my frame like earthquake. Ah me, I fear I am all too frail for this work. Yet dear is the love of life.

"*July 7.* — The last days I have passed in carefully searching the grounds, with the lens as before. Ul-Jabal constantly found pretexts for following me, and I am confident that every step I took was known to him. No sign anywhere of the grass having been disturbed. Yet my lands are wide, and I cannot be sure. The burden of this mighty task is greater than I can bear. I am weaker than a bruised reed. Shall I not slay my enemy, and make an end?

"*July 8.* — Ul-Jabal has been in my chamber again! I watched him through a crack in the panelling. His form was hidden by the bed, but I could see his hand reflected in the great mirror opposite the door. First, I cannot guess why, he moved to a point in front of the mirror the chair in which I sometimes sit. He then went to the box in which lie my few garments — and opened it. Ah, I have the stone — safe — safe! He fears my cunning, ancient eyes, and has hidden it in the one place where I would be least likely to seek it — *in my own trunk!* And yet I dread, most intensely I dread, to look.

"*July 9.* — The stone, alas, is not there! At the last moment he must have changed his purpose. Could his wondrous sensitiveness of intuition have made him feel that my eyes were looking in on him?

"*July 10.* — In the dead of night I knew that a stealthy foot had gone past my door. I rose and threw a mantle round me; I put on my head my cap of fur; I took the tempered blade in my hands; then crept out into the dark, and followed. Ul-Jabal carried a small lantern which revealed him to me. My feet were bare, but he wore felted slippers, which to my unfailing ear were not utterly noiseless. He descended the stairs to the bottom of the house, while I crouched behind him in the deepest gloom of the corners and walls. At the bottom he walked into the pantry: there stopped, and turned the lantern full in the direction of the spot where I stood; but so agilely did I slide behind a pillar, that he could not have seen me. In the pantry he lifted the trap-door, and descended still further into the vaults beneath the house. Ah, the vaults — the long, the tortuous, the darksome vaults — how had I forgotten them? Still I followed, rent by seismic shocks of terror. I had not forgotten the weapon: could I creep near enough, I felt that I might plunge it into the marrow of his back. He opened the iron door of the first vault and passed in. If I could lock him in? — but he held the key. On and on he wound his way, holding the lantern near the ground, his head bent down. The thought came to me *then,* that, had I but the courage, one swift sweep, and all were over. I crept closer, closer. Suddenly he turned round, and made a quick step in my direction. I saw his eyes, the murderous grin of his jaw. I know not if he saw me — thought forsook me. The weapon fell with clatter and clangor from my grasp, and in panic fright I fled with extended arms and the headlong swiftness of a stripling, through the black labyrinths of the caverns, through the vacant corridors of the house, till I reached my chamber, the door of which I had time to fasten on myself before I dropped, gasping, panting for very life, on the floor.

"*July 11.* — I had not the courage to see Ul-Jabal today. I have remained locked in my chamber all the time without food or water. My tongue cleaves to the roof of my mouth.

"*July 12.* — I took heart and crept downstairs. I met him in the study. He smiled on me, and I on him, as if nothing had happened between us. Oh, our old friendship, how it has turned into bitterest hate! I had taken the false stone from the Edmundsbury chalice and put it into the pocket of my brown gown, with the bold intention of showing it to him, and asking him if he knew aught of it. But when I faced him, my courage failed again. We drank together and ate together as in the old days of love.

"*July 13.* — I cannot think that I have not again imbibed some soporiferous drug. A great heaviness of sleep weighed on my brain till late in the day. When I woke my thoughts were in wild distraction, and a most peculiar condition of my skin held me fixed before the mirror. It is dry as parchment, and brown as the leaves of autumn.

"*July 14.* — Ul-Jabal is gone! And I am left a lonely, a desolate old man! He said, though I swore it was false, that I had grown to mistrust him! that I was hiding something from him! that he could live with me no more! No more, he said, should I see his face! The debt I owe him he would forgive. He has taken one small parcel with him, — and is gone!

"*July 15.* — Gone! gone! In mazeful dream I wander with uncovered head far and wide over my domain, seeking I know not what. The stone he has with him — the precious stone of Saul. I feel the life-surge ebbing, ebbing in my heart.''

Here the manuscript abruptly ended.

Prince Zaleski had listened as I read aloud, lying back on his Moorish couch and breathing slowly from his lips a heavy reddish vapor, which he imbibed from a very small, carved, bismuth pipette. His face, as far as I could see in the green-grey crepuscular atmosphere of the apartment, was expressionless. But when I had finished he turned fully round on me, and said:

"You perceive, I hope, the sinister meaning of all this?"

"*Has* it a meaning?"

Zaleski smiled.

"Can you doubt it? in the shape of a cloud, the pitch of a thrush's note, the *nuance* of a sea-shell you would find, had you only insight *enough,* inductive and deductive cunning *enough,* not only a meaning, but, I am convinced, a quite endless significance. Undoubtedly, in a human document of this kind, there is a meaning; and I may say at once that this meaning is entirely transparent to me. Pity only that you did not read the diary to me before."

"Why?"

"Because we might, between us, have prevented a crime, and saved a life. The last entry in the diary was made on the fifteenth of July. What day is this?"

"This is the twentieth."

"Then I would wager a thousand to one that we are too late. There is still, however, the one chance left. The time is now seven o'clock: seven of the evening, I think, not of the morning; the houses of business in London are therefore closed. But why not send my man, Ham, with a letter by train to the private address of the person from whom you obtained the diary, telling him to hasten immediately to Sir Jocelin Saul, and on no consideration to leave his side for a moment? Ham would reach this person before midnight, and understanding that the matter was one of life and death, he would assuredly do our bidding."

As I was writing the note suggested by Zaleski, I turned and asked him:

"From whom shall I say that the danger is to be expected — from the Indian?"

"From Ul-Jabal, yes; but by no means Indian — Persian."

Profoundly impressed by this knowledge of detail derived from sources which had brought me no intelligence, I handed the note to the negro, telling him how to proceed, and instructing him before starting from the station to search all the procurable papers of the last few days, and to return in case he found in any of them a notice of the death of Sir Jocelin Saul. Then I resumed my seat by the side of Zaleski.

"As I have told you," he said, "I am fully convinced that our messenger has gone on a bootless errand. I believe you will find that what has really occurred is this: either yesterday, or the day before, Sir Jocelin was found by his servant — I imagine he had a servant, though no mention is made of any — lying on the marble floor of his chamber, dead. Near him, probably by his side, will be found a gem — an oval stone, white in color — the same in fact which Ul-Jabal last placed in the Edmundsbury chalice. There will be no marks of violence — no trace of poison — the death will be found to be a perfectly natural one. Yet, in this case, a particularly wicked murder has been committed. There are, I assure you, to my positive knowledge forty-three — and in one island in the South Seas, forty-four — different methods of doing murder, any one of which would be entirely beyond the scope of the introspective agencies at the ordinary disposal of society.

"But let us bend our minds to the details of this matter. Let us ask first, *who* is this Ul-Jabal? I have said that he is a Persian, and of this there is abundant evidence in the narrative other than his mere name. Fragmentary as the document is, and not intended by the writer to afford the information, there is yet evidence of the religion of this man, of the particular sect of that religion to which he belonged, of his peculiar shade of color, of the object of his stay at the manor-house of Saul, of the special tribe amongst whom he formerly lived. 'What,' he asks, when his greedy eyes first light on the long-desired gem, 'what is the meaning of the inscription ''Has''' — the meaning which *he* so well knew. 'One of the lost secrets of the world,' replies the baronet. But I can hardly understand a learned Orientalist speaking in that way about what appears to me a very patent circumstance: it is clear that he never earnestly applied himself to the solution of the riddle, or else — what is more likely, in spite of his rather high-flown estimate of his own 'Reason' — that his mind, and the mind of his ancestors, never was able to go farther back in time than the Edmundsbury Monks. But *they* did not make the stone, nor did they dig it from the depths of the earth in Suffolk — they got it from someone, and it is not difficult to say with certainty from whom. The stone, then, might have been engraved by that someone, or by the someone from whom *he* received it, and so on back into the dimnesses of time. And consider the character of the engraving — it consists of *a mythological animal,* and some words, of which the letters 'Has' only are distinguishable. But the animal, at least, is pure Persian. The Persians, you know, were not only quite worthy competitors with the Hebrews, the Egyptians, and later on the Greeks, for excellence in the glyptic art, but this fact is remarkable, that in much the same way that the figure of the *scarabaeus* on an intaglio or cameo is a pretty infallible indication of an Egyptian hand, so is that of a priest or a grotesque animal a sure indication of a Persian. We may say, then, from that evidence alone — though there is more — that this gem was certainly Persian. And having reached that point, the mystery of 'Has' vanishes: for we at once jump at the conclusion that that too is Persian. But Persian, you say, written in English characters? Yes, and it was precisely this fact that made its meaning one of what the baronet childishly calls 'the lost secrets of the world': for every successive inquirer, believing it part of an English phrase, was thus hopelessly led astray in his investigation. 'Has' is, in fact, part of the word 'Hasn-us-Sabah,' and the mere circumstance that some of it has been obliterated, while the figure of the mystic animal remains intact, shows that it was executed by one of a nation less skilled in the art of graving in precious stones than the Persians — by a rude, mediaeval Englishman, in short — the modern revival of the art owing its origin, of course, to the Medici of a later age. And of this Englishman — who either graved the stone himself, or got someone else to do it for him — do we know nothing? We know, at least, that he was certainly a fighter, probably a Norman baron, that on his arm he bore the cross of red, that he trod the sacred soil of Palestine. Perhaps, to prove this, I need hardly remind you who Hasn-us-Sabah was. It is enough if I say that he was greatly mixed up in the affairs of the Crusaders, lending his irresistible arms now to this side, now to that. He was the chief of the heterodox Mohammedan sect of the Assassins (this word, I believe, is actually derived from his name); imagined himself to be an incarnation of the Deity, and from his inaccessible rock-fortress of Alamut in the Elburz exercised a sinister influence on the intricate politics of the day. The Red Cross

Knights called him Shaikh-ul-Jabal — the Old Man of the Mountains, that very nickname connecting him infallibly with the Ul-Jabal of our own times. Now three well-known facts occur to me in connection with this stone of the House of Saul: the first, that Saladin met in battle, and defeated, *and plundered,* in a certain place, on a certain day, this Hasn-us-Sabah, or one of his successors bearing the same name; the second, that about this time there was a cordial *rapprochement* between Saladin and Richard the Lion, and between the Infidels and the Christians generally, during which a free interchange of gems, then regarded as of deep mystic importance, took place — remember 'The Talisman,' and the 'Lee Penny'; the third, that soon after the fighters of Richard, and then himself, returned to England, the loculus or coffin of St. Edmund (as we are informed by the *Jocelini Chronica*) was *opened by the Abbot* at midnight, and the body of the martyr exposed. On such occasions it was customary to place gems and relics in the coffin, when it was again closed up. Now, the chalice with the stone was taken from this loculus; and is it possible not to believe that some knight, to whom it had been presented by one of Saladin's men, had in turn presented it to the monastery, first scratching uncouthly on its surface the name of Hasn to mark its semi-sacred origin, or perhaps bidding the monks to do so? But the Assassins, now called, I think, 'al Hasani' or 'Ismaili' — 'that accursed *Ishmaelite,*' the baronet exclaims in one place — still live, are still a flourishing sect impelled by fervid religious fanaticisms. And where think you is their chief place of settlement? Where, but on the heights of that same 'Lebanon' on which Sir Jocelin 'picked up' his too doubtful scribe and literary helper?

"It now becomes evident that Ul-Jabal was one of the sect of the Assassins, and that the object of his sojourn at the manor-house, of his financial help to the baronet, of his whole journey perhaps to England, was the recovery of the sacred gem which once glittered on the breast of the founder of his sect. In dread of spoiling all by over-rashness, he waits, perhaps for years, till he makes sure that the stone is the right one by seeing it with his own eyes, and learns the secret of the spring by which the chalice is opened. He then proceeds to steal it. So far all is clear enough. Now, this too is conceivable, that, intending to commit the theft, he had beforehand provided himself with another stone similar in size and shape — these being well known to him — to the other, in order to substitute it for the real stone, and so, for a time at least, escape detection. It is presumable that the chalice was not often *opened* by the baronet, and this would therefore have been a perfectly rational device on the part of Ul-Jabal. But assuming this to be his mode of thinking, how ludicrously absurd appears all the trouble he took to *engrave* the false stone in an exactly similar manner to the other. *That* could not help him in producing the deception, for that he did not contemplate the stone being *seen,* but only *heard* in the cup, is proved by the fact that he selected a stone of a different *color.* This color, as I shall afterwards show you, was that of a pale, brown-spotted stone. But we are met with something more extraordinary still when we come to the last stone, the white one — I shall prove that it was white — which Ul-Jabal placed in the cup. Is it possible that he had provided *two* substitutes, and that he had engraved these *two,* without object, in the same minutely careful manner? Your mind refuses to conceive it; and *having* done this, declines, in addition, to believe that he had prepared even one substitute; and I am fully in accord with you in this conclusion.

"We may say then that Ul-Jabal had not *prepared* any substitute; and it may be added that it was a thing altogether beyond the limits of the probable that he could *by chance* have possessed two old gems exactly similar in every detail down to the very half-obliterated letters of the word 'Hasn-us-Sabah.' I have now shown, you perceive, that he did not make them purposely, and that he did not possess them accidentally. Nor were they the baronet's, for we have his declaration that he had never seen them before. When then did the Persian obtain them? That point will immediately emerge into clearness, when we have sounded his motive for replacing the one false stone by the other, and, above all, for taking away the valueless stone, and then replacing it. And in order to lead you up to the comprehension of this motive, I begin by making the bold assertion that Ul-Jabal had not in his possession the real St. Edmundsbury stone at all.

"You are surprised; for you argue that if we are to take the baronet's evidence at all, we must take it in this particular also, and he positively asserts that he saw the Persian take the stone. It is true that there are indubitable signs of insanity in the document, but it is the insanity of a diseased mind manifesting itself by fantastic exaggeration of sentiment, rather than of a mind confiding to itself its own delusions as to matters of fact. There is therefore nothing so certain as that Ul-Jabal did steal the gem; but these two things are equally evident: that by some means or other it very soon passed out of his possession, and that when it had so passed, he, for his part, believed it to be in the possession of the baronet. 'Now,' he cries in triumph, one day as he catches Sir Jocelin in his room — '*now* you have delivered all into my hands.' 'All' what, Sir Jocelin wonders.

'All,' of course, meant the stone. He believes that the baronet has done precisely what the baronet afterwards believes that *he* has done — hidden away the stone in the most secret of all places, in his own apartment, to wit. The Persian, sure now at last of victory, accordingly hastens into his chamber, and 'locks the door,' in order, by an easy search, to secure his prize. When, moreover, the baronet is examining the house at night with his lens, he believes that Ul-Jabal is spying his movements; when he extends his operations to the park, the other finds pretexts to be near him. Ul-Jabal dogs his footsteps like a shadow. But supposing he had really had the jewel, and had deposited it in a place of perfect safety — such as, with or without lenses, the extensive grounds of the manor-house would certainly have afforded — his more reasonable *rôle* would have been that of unconscious *nonchalance,* rather than of agonized interest. But, in fact, he supposed the owner of the stone to be himself seeking a secure hiding-place for it, and is resolved at all costs on knowing the secret. And again in the vaults beneath the house Sir Jocelin reports that Ul-Jabal 'holds the lantern near the ground, with his head bent down': can anything be better descriptive of the attitude of *search?* Yet each is so sure that the other possesses the gem, that neither is able to suspect that both are seekers.

''But, after all, there is far better evidence of the non-possession of the stone by the Persian than all this — and that is the murder of the baronet, for I can almost promise you that our messenger will return in a few minutes. Now, it seems to me that Ul-Jabal was not really murderous, averse rather to murder; thus the baronet is often in his power, swoons in his arms, lies under the influence of narcotics in semi-sleep while the Persian is in his room, and yet no injury is done him. Still, when the clear necessity to murder — the clear means of gaining the stone — presents itself to Ul-Jabal, he does not hesitate a moment — indeed, he has already made elaborate preparations for that very necessity. And when was it that this necessity presented itself? It was when the baronet put the false stone in the pocket of a loose gown for the purpose of confronting the Persian with it. But what kind of pocket? I think you will agree with me, that male garments, admitting of the designation 'gown,' have usually only outer pockets — large, square pockets, simply sewed on to the outside of the robe. But a stone of that size *must* have made such a pocket bulge outwards. Ul-Jabal must have noticed it. Never before has he been perfectly sure that the baronet carried the long-desired gem about on his body; but now at last he knows beyond all doubt. To obtain it, there are several courses open to him: he may rush there and then on the weak old man and tear the stone from him; he may ply him with narcotics, and extract it from the pocket during sleep. But in these there is a small chance of failure; there is a certainty of near or ultimate detection, pursuit — and this is a land of law, swift and fairly sure. No, the old man must die: only thus — thus surely, and thus secretly — can the outraged dignity of Hasn-us-Sabah be appeased. On the very next day he leaves the house — no more shall the mistrustful baronet, who is 'hiding something from him,' see his face. He carries with him a small parcel. Let me tell you what was in that parcel: it contained the baronet's fur cap, one of his 'brown gowns,' and a snow-white beard and wig. Of the cap we can be sure; for from the fact that, on leaving his room at midnight to follow the Persian through the *house,* he put it on his head, I gather that he wore it habitually during all his waking hours; yet after Ul-Jabal has left him he wanders *far and wide* 'with uncovered head.' Can you not picture the distracted old man seeking ever and anon with absent mind for his long-accustomed head-gear, and seeking in vain? Of the gown, too, we may be equally certain: for it was the procuring of this that led Ul-Jabal to the baronet's trunk; we now know that he did not go there to *hide* the stone, for he had it not to hide; nor to *seek* it, for he would be unable to believe the baronet childish enough to deposit it in so obvious a place. As for the wig and beard, they had been previously seen in his room. But before he leaves the house Ul-Jabal has one more work to do: once more the two eat and drink together as in 'the old days of love'; once more the baronet is drunken with a deep sleep, and when he wakes, his skin is 'brown as the leaves of autumn.' That is the evidence of which I spoke in the beginning as giving us a hint of the exact shade of the Oriental's color — it was the yellowish-brown of a sered leaf. And now that the face of the baronet has been smeared with this indelible pigment, all is ready for the tragedy, and Ul-Jabal departs. He will return, but not immediately, for he will at least give the eyes of his victim time to grow accustomed to the change of color in his face; nor will he tarry long, for there is no telling whether, or whither, the stone may not disappear from that outer pocket. I therefore surmise that the tragedy took place a day or two ago. I remembered the feebleness of the old man, his highly neurotic condition; I thought of those 'fibrillary twitchings,' indicating the onset of a well-known nervous disorder sure to end in sudden death; I recalled his belief that on account of the loss of the stone, in which he felt his life bound up, the chariot of death was urgent on his footsteps; I bore in mind his memory of his grandfather dying in agony just seventy years ago after seeing his own wraith by the churchyard-wall; I knew that such a man could not be struck by the sudden, the terrific shock of seeing *himself* sitting in the chair before the mirror (the chair, you remember, had been *placed* there by Ul-Jabal) without dropping down stone dead on the spot. I was thus able to predict the manner and place of the baronet's death — if he *be* dead. Beside him, I said, would probably be found a white stone. For Ul-Jabal, his ghastly impersonation ended, would hurry to the pocket, snatch out the stone, and finding it not the stone he sought, would in all likelihood dash it down, fly away from the corpse as if from plague, and, I hope, straightway go and — hang himself.''

It was at this point that the black mask of Ham framed itself between the python-skin tapestries of the doorway. I tore from him the paper, now two days old, which he held in his hand, and under the heading, ''Sudden death of a Baronet,'' read a nearly exact account of the facts which Zaleski had been detailing to me.

''I can see by your face that I was not altogether at fault,'' he said, with one of his musical laughs; ''but there still remains for us to discover whence Ul-Jabal obtained his two substitutes, his motive for exchanging one for the other, and for stealing the valueless gem; but, above all, we must find where the real stone was all the time that these two men so sedulously sought it, and where it now is. Now, let us turn our attention to this stone, and ask, first, what light does the inscription on the cup throw on its nature? The inscription assures us that if 'this stone be stolen,' or if it 'chaunges dre,' the House of Saul and its head 'anoon' (*i.e.* anon, at once) shall die. 'Dre,' I may remind you, is an old English word, used, I think, by Burns, identical with the Saxon *'dreogan,'* meaning to 'suffer.' So that the writer at least contemplated that the stone might 'suffer changes.' But what kind of changes — external or internal? External change — change of environment — is already provided for when he says, 'shulde this Ston stalen bee'; 'chaunges,' therefore, in *his* mind, meant internal changes. But is such a thing possible for any precious stone, and for this one in particular? As to that, we might answer when we know the name of this one. It nowhere appears in the manuscript, and yet it is immediately discoverable. For it was a 'sky-blue' stone; a sky-blue, sacred stone; a sky-blue, sacred, Persian stone. That at once gives us its name — it was a *turquoise.* But can the turquoise, to the certain knowledge of a mediaeval writer, 'chaunges dre'? Let us turn for light to old Anselm de Boot: that is he in pig-skin on the shelf behind the bronze Hera.''

I handed the volume to Zaleski. He pointed to a passage which read as follows:

''Assuredly the turquoise doth possess a soul more intelligent than that of man. But we cannot be wholly sure of the presence of Angels in precious stones. I do rather opine that the evil spirit doth take up his abode therein, transforming himself into an angel of light, to the end that we put our trust not in God, but in the precious stone; and thus, perhaps, doth he deceive our spirits by the turquoise: for the turquoise is of two sorts: those which keep their color, and those which lose it.''*

*''Assurément la turquoise à une ame plus intelligente que l'ame de l'homme. Mais nous ne pouvons rien establir de certain touchant la presence des Anges dans les pierres precieuses. Mon jugement seroit plustot que le mauvais esprit, qui se transforme en Ange de lumiere se loge dans les pierres precieuses, à fin que l'on ne recoure pas à Dieu, mais que l'on repose sa creance dans la pierre precieuse; ainsi, peut-être, il deçoit nos esprits par la turquoise: car la turquoise est de deux sortes, les unes qui conservent leur couleur et les autres qui la perdent.'' — *Anselm de Boot,* Book II.

"You thus see," resumed Zaleski, "that the turquoise was believed to have the property of changing its color — a change which was universally supposed to indicate the fading away and death of its owner. The good de Boot, alas, believed this to be a property of too many other stones beside, like the Hebrews in respect of their urim and thummim; but in the case of the turquoise, at least, it is a well-authenticated natural phenomenon, and I have myself seen such a specimen. In some cases the change is a gradual process; in others it may occur suddenly within an hour, especially when the gem, long kept in the dark, is exposed to brilliant sunshine. I should say, however, that in this metamorphosis there is always an intermediate stage: the stone first changes from blue to a pale color spotted with brown, and, lastly, to a pure white. Thus, Ul-Jabal having stolen the stone, finds that it is of the wrong color, and soon after replaces it; he supposes that in the darkness he has selected the wrong chalice, and so takes the valueless stone from the other. This, too, he replaces, and, infinitely puzzled, makes yet another hopeless trial of the Edmundsbury chalice, and, again baffled, again replaces it, concluding now that the baronet has suspected his designs, and substituted a false stone for the real one. But *after* this last replacement, the stone assumes its final hue of white, and thus the baronet is led to think that two stones have been substituted by Ul-Jabal for his own invaluable gem. All this while the gem was lying serenely in its place in the chalice. And thus it came to pass that in the manor-house of Saul there arose a somewhat considerable Ado about Nothing."

For a moment Zaleski paused; then, turning round and laying his hand on the brown forehead of the mummy by his side, he said:

"My friend here could tell you, and he would, a fine tale of the immensely important part which jewels in all ages have played in human history, human religions, institutions, ideas. He flourished some five centuries before the Messiah, was a Memphian priest of Amsu, and, as the hieroglyphics on his coffin assure me, a prime favorite with one Queen Amyntas. Beneath these mouldering swaddlings of the grave a great ruby still cherishes its blood-guilty secret on the forefinger of his right hand. Most curious is it to reflect how in *all* lands, and at *all* times, precious minerals have been endowed by men with mystic virtues. The Persians, for instance, believed that spinelle and the garnet were harbingers of joy. Have you read the ancient Bishop of Rennes on the subject? Really, I almost think there must be some truth in all this. The instinct of universal man is rarely far at fault. Already you have a semi-comic 'gold-cure' for alcoholism, and you have heard of the geophagism of certain African tribes. What if the scientist of the future be destined to discover that the diamond, and it alone, is a specific for cholera, that powdered rubellite cures fever, and the chrysoberyl gout? It would be in exact conformity with what I have hitherto observed of a general trend towards a certain inborn perverseness and whimsicality in Nature.''

Note. — As some proof of the fineness of intuition evidenced by Zaleski, as distinct from his more conspicuous powers of reasoning, I may here state that some years after the occurrence of the tragedy I have recorded above, the skeleton of a man was discovered in the vaults of the manor-house of Saul. I have not the least doubt that it was the skeleton of Ul-Jabal. The teeth were very prominent. A rotten rope was found loosely knotted round the vertebrae of his neck.

The S.S.

Wohlgeborne, gesunde Kinder bringen viel mit. . . . Wenn die Natur verabscheut, so spricht sie es laut aus: das Geschöpf, das falsch lebt, wird früh zerstört. Unfruchtbarkeit, kümmerliches Dasein, frühzeitiges Zerfallen, das sind ihre Flüche, die Kennzeichen ihrer Strenge.*

—GOETHE

"Ἄργος δὲ ἀνδρῶν ἐχηρώθη οὕτω ὥστε οἱ δοῦλοι αὐτῶν ἔσχον πάντα τὰ πρήγματα ἄρχοντές τε καὶ διέποντες, ἐς ὃ ἐπήβησαν οἱ τῶν ἀπολομένων παῖδες.**"

—HERODOTUS

To say that there are epidemics of suicide is to give expression to what is now a mere commonplace of knowledge. And so far are they from being of rare occurrence, that it has even been affirmed that every sensational case of *felo de se* published in the newspapers is sure to be followed by some others more obscure: their frequency, indeed, is out of all proportion with the *extent* of each particular outbreak. Sometimes, however, especially in villages and small townships, the wildfire madness becomes an

* Well-made, healthy children bring much into the world along with them. . . . When Nature abhors, she speaks it aloud: the creature that lives with a false life is soon destroyed. Unfruitfulness, painful existence, early destruction, these are her curses, the tokens of her displeasure.

** And Argos was so depleted of Men (i.e. *after the battle with Cleomenes*) that the slaves usurped everything — ruling and disposing — until such time as the sons of the slain were grown up.

67

all-involving passion, emulating in its fury the great plagues of history. Of such kind was the craze in Versailles in 1793, when about a quarter of the whole population perished by the scourge; while that at the *Hôtel des Invalides* in Paris was only a notable one of the many which have occurred during the present century. At such times it is as if the optic nerve of the mind throughout whole communities became distorted, till in the noseless and black-robed Reaper it discerned an angel of very loveliness. As a brimming maiden, out-worn by her virginity, yields half-fainting to the dear sick stress of her desire — with just such faintings, wanton fires, does the soul, over-taxed by the continence of living, yield voluntary to the grave, and adulterously make of Death its paramour.

> "When she sees a bank
> Stuck full of flowers, she, with a sigh, will tell
> Her servants, what a pretty place it were
> To bury lovers in; and make her maids
> Pluck 'em, and strew her over like a corse."*

The *mode* spreads — then rushes into rage: to breathe is to be obsolete: to wear the shroud becomes *comme il faut,* this cerecloth acquiring all the attractiveness and *éclat* of a wedding-garment. The coffin is not too strait for lawless nuptial bed; and the sweet clods of the valley will prove no barren bridegroom of a writhing progeny. There is, however, nothing specially mysterious in the operation of a pestilence of this nature: it is as conceivable, if not yet as explicable, as the contagion of cholera,

* Beaumont and Fletcher: *The Maid's Tragedy.*

mind being at least as sensitive to the touch of mind as body to that of body.

It was during the ever-memorable outbreak of this obscure malady in the year 1875 that I ventured to break in on the calm of that deep Silence in which, as in a mantle, my friend Prince Zaleski had wrapped himself. I wrote, in fact, to ask him what he thought of the epidemic. His answer was in the laconic words addressed to the Master in the house of woe at Bethany:

"Come and see."

To this, however, he added in postscript: "But what epidemic?"

I had momentarily lost sight of the fact that Zaleski had so absolutely cut himself off from the world, that he was not in the least likely to know anything even of the appalling series of events to which I had referred. And yet it is no exaggeration to say that those events had thrown the greater part of Europe into a state of consternation, and even confusion. In London, Manchester, Paris, and Berlin, especially the excitement was intense. On the Sunday preceding the writing of my note to Zaleski, I was present at a monster demonstration held in Hyde Park, in which the Government was held up on all hands to the popular derision and censure — for it will be remembered that to many minds the mysterious accompaniments of some of the deaths daily occurring conveyed a still darker significance than that implied in mere self-destruction, and seemed to point to a succession of purposeless and hideous murders. The demagogues, I must say, spoke with some wildness and incoherence. Many laid the blame at the door of the police, and urged that things would be different were *they* but placed under municipal, instead of under imperial, control. A thousand panaceas were invented, a

thousand aimless censures passed. But the people listened with
vacant ear. Never have I seen the populace so agitated, and yet
so subdued, as with the sense of some impending doom. The
glittering eye betrayed the excitement, the pallor of the cheek
the doubt, the haunting *fear*. None felt himself quite safe; men
recognized shuddering the grin of death in the air. To tingle
with affright, and to know not why — that is the tran-
scendentalism of terror. The threat of the cannon's mouth is
trivial in its effect on the mind in comparison with the menace
of a Shadow. It is the pestilence that walketh *by night* that is in-
tolerable. As for myself, I confess to being pervaded with a
nameless and numbing awe during all those weeks. And this
feeling appeared to be general in the land. The journals had but
one topic; the party organs threw politics to the winds. I heard
that on the Stock Exchange, as in the Paris *Bourse,* business
decreased to a minimum. In Parliament the work of law-
threshing practically ceased, and the time of Ministers was
nightly spent in answering volumes of angry ''Questions,'' and
in facing motion after motion for the ''adjournment'' of the
House.

It was in the midst of all this commotion that I received Prince
Zaleski's brief ''Come and see.'' I was flattered and pleased:
flattered, because I suspected that to me alone, of all men, would
such an invitation, coming from him, be addressed; and pleased,
because many a time in the midst of the noisy city street and the
garish, dusty world, had the thought of that vast mansion, that
dim and silent chamber, flooded my mind with a drowsy sense of
the romantic, till, from very excess of melancholy sweetness in
the picture, I was fain to close my eyes. I avow that that
lonesome room — gloomy in its lunar bath of soft perfumed
light — shrouded in the sullen voluptuousness of plushy, nar-

cotic-breathing draperies — pervaded by the mysterious spirit of its brooding occupant — grew more and more on my fantasy, till the remembrance had for me all the cool refreshment shed by a midsummer-night's dream in the dewy deeps of some Perrhaebian grove of cornel and lotos and ruby stars of the asphodel. It was, therefore, in all haste that I set out to share for a time in the solitude of my friend.

Zaleski's reception of me was most cordial; immediately on my entrance into his sanctum he broke into a perfect torrent of wild, enthusiastic words, telling me with a kind of rapture, that he was just then laboriously engaged in co-ordinating to one of the calculi certain new properties he had discovered in the parabola, adding with infinite gusto his ''firm'' belief that the ancient Assyrians were acquainted with all our modern notions respecting the parabola itself, the projection of bodies in general, and of the heavenly bodies in particular; and must, moreover, from certain inferences of his own in connection with the Winged Circle, have been conversant with the fact that light is not an ether, but only the vibration of an ether. He then galloped on to suggest that I should at once take part with him in his investigations, and commented on the timeliness of my visit. I, on my part, was anxious for his opinion on other and far weightier matters than the concerns of the Assyrians, and intimated as much to him. But for two days he was firm in his tacit refusal to listen to my story; and, concluding that he was disinclined to undergo the agony of unrest with which he was always tormented by any mystery which momentarily baffled him, I was, of course, forced to hold my peace. On the third day, however, of his own accord he asked me to what epidemic I had referred. I then detailed to him some of the strange events which were agitating the mind of the outside world. From the very first he was interested: later on that interest grew into a passion, a greedy soul-consuming quest after the truth, the intensity of which was such at least as to move me even to pity.

I may as well here restate the facts as I communicated them to Zaleski. The concatenation of incidents, it will be remembered, started with the extraordinary death of that eminent man of science, Professor Schleschinger, consulting laryngologist to the *Charité* Hospital in Berlin. The professor, a man of great age, was on the point of contracting his third marriage with the beautiful and accomplished daughter of the Herr Geheimrath Otto von Friedrich. The contemplated union, which was entirely one of those *mariages de convenance* so common in good society, sprang out of the professor's ardent desire to leave behind him a direct heir to his very considerable wealth. By his first two marriages, indeed, he had had large families, and was at this very time surrounded by quite an army of little grandchildren, from whom (all his direct descendants being dead) he might have been content to select his heir; but the old German prejudices in these matters are strong, and he still hoped to be represented on his decease by a son of his own. To this whim the charming Ottilie was marked by her parents as the victim. The wedding, however, had been postponed owing to a slight illness of the veteran scientist, and just as he was on the point of final recovery from it, death intervened to prevent altogether the execution of his design. Never did death of man create a profounder sensation; *never was death of man followed by consequences more terrible.* The *Residenz* of the scientist was a stately mansion near the University in the *Unter den Linden* boulevard, that is to say, in the most fashionable *Quartier* of Berlin. His bedroom from a considerable height looked out on a small back garden, and in this room he had been engaged in conversation with his colleague and medical attendant, Dr. Johann Hofmeier, to a late hour of the night. During all this time he seemed cheerful, and spoke quite lucidly on various topics. In particular, he exhibited to his colleague a curious strip of what looked like ancient papyrus, on which were traced certain grotesque and apparently meaningless figures. This, he said, he had found some days before on the bed of a poor woman in one of the horribly low quarters that surround Berlin, on whom he had had occasion to make a *post-mortem* examination. The woman had suffered from partial paralysis. She had a small young family, none of whom, however, could give any account of the slip, except one little girl, who declared that she had taken it ''from her mother's mouth'' after death. The slip was soiled, and had a fragrant smell, as though it had been smeared with honey. The professor added that all through his illness he had been employing himself by examining these figures. He was convinced, he said, that they contained some archaeological significance; but, in any case, he ceased not to ask himself how came a slip of papyrus to be found in such a situation — on the bed of a dead Berlinerin of the poorest class? The story of its being taken from the *mouth* of the woman was, of course, unbelievable. The whole incident seemed to puzzle, while it amused him; seemed to appeal to the instinct — so strong in him — to investigate, to probe. For days, he declared, he had been endeavoring, in vain, to make anything of the figures. Dr. Hofmeier, too, examined the slip, but inclined to believe that the figures — rude and uncouth as they were — were only such as might be drawn by any schoolboy in an idle moment. They consisted merely of a man and a woman seated on a bench, with what looked like an ornamental border running round them. After a pleasant evening's scientific gossip, Dr. Hofmeier, a little after midnight, took his departure from the bedside. An hour later the servants were roused from sleep by one deep, raucous cry proceeding from the professor's room. They hastened to his door; it was locked on the inside; all was still within. No answer coming to their calls, the door was broken in. They found their master lying calm and dead on his bed. A window of the room was open, but there was nothing to show that anyone had entered it. Dr. Hofmeier was sent for, and was soon on the scene. After examining the body, he failed to find anything to account for the sudden demise of his old friend and chief. One observation, however, had the effect of causing him to tingle with horror. On his entrance he had noticed, lying on the side of the bed, the piece of papyrus with which the professor had been toying in the earlier part of the day, and had removed it. But, as he was on the point of leaving the room, he happened to approach the corpse once more, and bending over it, noticed that the lips and teeth were slightly parted. Drawing open the now stiffened jaws, he found — to his amazement, to his stupefaction — that, neatly folded beneath the dead tongue, lay just another piece of papyrus as that which he had removed from the bed. He drew it out — it was clammy. He put it to his nose — it exhaled the fragrance of honey. He opened it — it was covered by figures. He compared them with the figures on the other slip — they were just so similar as two draftsmen hastily copying from a common model would make them. The doctor was unnerved: he hurried homeward, and immediately submitted the honey on the papyrus to a rigorous chemical analysis: he suspected poison — a subtle poison — as the means of a suicide, grotesquely, insanely accomplished. He found the fluid to be perfectly innocuous — pure honey, and nothing more.

The next day Germany thrilled with the news that Professor Schleschinger had destroyed himself. For suicide, however, some of the papers substituted murder, though of neither was there an atom of actual proof. On the day following, three persons died by their own hands in Berlin, of whom two were young members of the medical profession; on the day following that, the number rose to nineteen, Hamburg, Dresden, and Aachen joining in the frenzied death-dance; within three weeks from the night on which Professor Schleschinger met his unaccountable end, eight thousand persons in Germany, France, and Great Britain, died in that startlingly sudden and secret manner which we call ''tragic,'' many of them obviously by their own hands, many, in what seemed the servility of a fatal imitativeness, with figured, honey-smeared slips of papyrus beneath their tongues. Even now — now, after years — I thrill intensely to recall the dread remembrance; but to live through it, to breathe daily the mawkish, miasmatic atmosphere, all vapid with the suffocating death — ah, it was terror too deep, nausea too foul, for mortal bearing. Novalis has somewhere hinted at the possibility (or the desirability) of a simultaneous suicide and voluntary return by the whole human family into the sweet bosom of our ancient Father — I half expected it was coming, had come, *then*. It was as if the old, good-easy, meek-eyed man of science, dying, had left his effectual curse on all the world, and had thereby converted civilization into one omnivorous grave, one universal charnel-house.

I spent several days in reading out to Zaleski accounts of particular deaths as they had occurred. He seemed never to tire of listening, lying back for the most part on the silver-cushioned couch, and wearing an inscrutable mask. Sometimes he rose and paced the carpet with noiseless footfall, his steps increasing to the swaying, uneven velocity of an animal in confinement as a passage here or there attracted him, and then subsiding into their slow regularity again. At any interruption in the reading, he would instantly turn to me with a certain impatience, and implore me to proceed; and when our stock of matter failed, he broke out into actual anger that I had not brought more with me. Henceforth the negro, Ham, using my trap, daily took a double journey — one before sunrise, and one at dusk — to the nearest townlet, from which he would return loaded with newspapers. With unimaginable eagerness did both Zaleski and I seize, morning after morning, and evening after evening, on these budgets, to gloat for long hours over the ever-lengthening tale of death. As for him, sleep forsook him. He was a man of small reasonableness, scorning the limitations of human capacity; his palate brooked no meat when his brain was headlong in the chase; even the mild narcotics which were now his food and drink seemed to lose something of their power to mollify, to curb him. Often rising from slumber in what I took to be the dead of night — though of day or night there could be small certainty in that dim dwelling — I would peep into the domed chamber, and see him there under the livid-green light of the censer, the leaden smoke issuing from his lips, his eyes fixed unweariedly on a square piece of ebony which rested on the coffin of the mummy near him. On this ebony he had pasted side by side several woodcuts — snipped from the newspapers — of the figures traced on the pieces of papyrus found in the mouths of the dead. I could see, as time passed, that he was concentrating all his powers on these figures; for the details of the deaths themselves were all of a dreary sameness, offering few salient points for investigation. In those cases where the suicide had left behind him clear evidence of the means by which he had committed the act, there was nothing to investigate; the others — rich and poor alike, peer and peasant — trooped out by thousands on the far journey, without leaving the faintest footprint to mark the road by which they had gone.

This was perhaps the reason that, after a time, Zaleski discarded the newspapers, leaving their perusal to me, and turned his attention exclusively to the ebon tablet. Knowing as I full well did the daring and success of his past spiritual adventures — the subtlety, the imagination, the imperial grip of his intellect — I did not at all doubt that his choice was wise, and would in the end be justified. These woodcuts — now so notorious — were all exactly similar in design, though minutely differing here and there in drawing. The following is a facsimile of one of them taken by me at random:

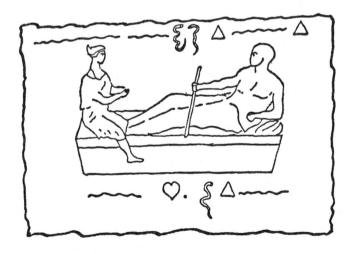

The time passed. It now began to be a grief to me to see the turgid pallor that gradually overspread the always ashen countenance of Zaleski; I grew to consider the ravaging life that glared and blazed in his sunken eye as too volcanic, demonic, to be canny: the mystery, I decided at last — if mystery there were — was too deep, too dark, for him. Hence perhaps it was, that I now absented myself more and more from him in the adjoining room in which I slept. There one day I sat reading over the latest list of horrors, when I heard a loud cry from the vaulted chamber. I rushed to the door and beheld him standing, gazing with wild eyes at the ebon tablet held straight out in front of him.

"By Heaven!" he cried, stamping savagely with his foot. "By Heaven! Then I certainly *am* a fool! *It is the staff of Phoebus in the hand of Hermes!*"

I hastened to him. "Tell me," I said, "have you discovered anything?"

"It is possible."

"And has there really been foul play — murder — in any of these deaths?"

"Of that, at least, I was certain from the first."

"Great God!" I exclaimed, "Could any son of man so convert himself into a fiend, a beast of the wilderness ——"

"You judge precisely in the manner of the multitude," he answered somewhat petulantly. "Illegal murder is always a mistake, but not necessarily a crime. Remember Corday. But in cases where the murder of one is really fiendish, why is it qualitatively less fiendish than the murder of many? On the other hand, had Brutus slain a thousand Caesars — each act involving an additional exhibition of the sublimest self-suppression — he might well have taken rank as a saint in heaven."

Failing for the moment to see the drift or the connection of the argument, I contented myself with waiting events. For the rest of that day and the next Zaleski seemed to have dismissed the matter of the tragedies from his mind, and entered calmly on his former studies. He no longer consulted the news, or examined the figures on the tablet. The papers, however, still arrived daily, and of these he soon afterwards laid several before me, pointing, with a curious smile, to a small paragraph in each. These all appeared in the advertisement columns, were worded alike, and read as follows: —

"A true son of Lycurgus, *having news,* desires to know the *time* and *place* of the next meeting of his Phyle. Address Zaleski, at R—— Abbey, in the county of M——."

I gazed in mute alternation at the advertisement and at him. I may here stop to make mention of a very remarkable sensation which my association with him occasionally produced in me. I felt it with intense, with unpleasant, with irritating keenness at this moment. It was the sensation of being borne aloft — aloft — by a force external to myself — such a sensation as might possibly tingle through an earthworm when lifted into illimitable airy heights by the strongly-daring pinions of an eagle. It was the feeling of being hurried out beyond one's depth — caught and whiffed away by the all-compelling sweep of some rabid vigor into a new, foreign element. Something akin I have experienced in an "express" as it raged with me — winged, rocking, ecstatic, shrilling a dragon Aha! — round a too narrow curve. It was a sensation very far from agreeable.

"To that," he said, pointing to the paragraph, "we may, I

think, shortly expect an answer. Let us only hope that when it comes it may be immediately intelligible.''

We waited throughout the whole of that day and night, hiding our eagerness under the pretence of absorption in our books. If by chance I fell into an uneasy doze, I found him on waking ever watchful, and poring over the great tome before him. About the time, however, when, could we have seen it, the first grey of dawn must have been peeping over the land, his impatience again became painful to witness: he rose and paced the room, muttering occasionally to himself. This only ceased, when, hours later, Ham entered the room with an envelope in his hand. Zaleski seized it — tore it open — ran his eye over the contents — and dashed *it* to the ground with an oath.

''Curse it!'' he groaned. ''Ah, curse it! unintelligible — every syllable of it!''

I picked up the missive and examined it. It was a slip of papyrus covered with the design now so hideously familiar, except only that the two central figures were wanting. At the bottom was written the date of the fifteenth of November — it was then the morning of the twelfth — and the name ''Morris.'' The whole, therefore, presented the following appearance:

My eyes were now heavy with sleep, every sense half-drunken with the vaporlike atmosphere of the room, so that, having abandoned something of hope, I tottered willingly to my bed, and fell into a profound slumber, which lasted till what must have been the time of the gathering in of the shades of night. I then rose. Missing Zaleski, I sought through all the chambers for him. He was nowhere to be seen. The negro informed me with an affectionate and anxious tremor in his voice that his master had left the rooms some hours before, but had said nothing to him. I ordered the man to descend and look into the sacristy of the small chapel wherein I had deposited my *calèche,* and in the field behind, where my horse should be. He returned with the news that both had disappeared. Zaleski, I then concluded, had undoubtedly departed on a journey.

I was deeply touched by the demeanor of Ham as the hours went by. He wandered stealthily about the rooms like a lost being. It was like matter sighing after, weeping over, spirit. Prince Zaleski had never before withdrawn himself from the *surveillance* of this sturdy watchman, and his disappearance now was like a convulsion in their little cosmos. Ham implored me repeatedly, if I could, to throw some light on the meaning of this catastrophe. But I too was in the dark. The titanic frame of the Ethiopian trembled with emotion as in broken, childish words he told me that he felt instinctively the approach of some great danger to the person of his master. So a day passed away, and then another. On the next he roused me from sleep to hand me a letter which, on opening, I found to be from Zaleski. It was hastily scribbled in pencil, dated "London, Nov. 14th," and ran thus:

"For my body — should I not return by Friday night — you will, no doubt, be good enough to make search. *Descend* the river, keeping constantly to the left; consult the papyrus; and stop at the *Descensus AEsopi.* Seek diligently, and you will find. For the rest, you know my fancy for cremation: take me, if you will, to the crematorium of *Père-Lachaise.* My whole fortune I decree to Ham, the Lybian.''

Ham was all for knowing the contents of this letter, but I refused to communicate a word of it. I was dazed, I was more than ever perplexed, I was appalled by the frenzy of Zaleski. Friday night! It was then Thursday morning. And I was expected to wait through the dreary interval uncertain, agonized, inactive! I was offended with my friend; his conduct bore the interpretation of mental distraction. The leaden hours passed all oppressively while I sought to appease the keenness of my unrest with the anodyne of drugged sleep. On the next morning, however, another letter — a rather massive one — reached me. The covering was directed in the writing of Zaleski, but on it he had scribbled the words: ''This need not be opened unless I fail to reappear before Saturday.'' I therefore laid the packet aside unread.

I waited all through Friday, resolved that at six o'clock, if nothing happened, I should make some sort of effort. But from six I remained, with eyes strained towards the doorway, until ten. I was so utterly at a loss, my ingenuity was so entirely baffled by the situation, that I could devise no course of action which did not immediately appear absurd. But at midnight I sprang up — no longer would I endure the carking suspense. I seized a taper, and passed through the doorway. I had not proceeded far, however, when my light was extinguished. Then I remembered with a shudder that I should have to pass through the whole vast length of the building in order to gain an exit. It was an all but hopeless task in the profound darkness to thread my way through the labyrinth of halls and corridors, of tumble-down stairs, of bat-haunted vaults, of purposeless angles and involutions; but I proceeded with something of a blind obstinacy, groping my way with arms held out before me. In this manner I had wandered on for perhaps a quarter of an hour, when my fingers came into distinct momentary contact with what felt like cold and humid human flesh. I shrank back, unnerved as I already was, with a murmur of affright.

"Zaleski?" I whispered with bated breath.

Intently as I strained my ears, I could detect no reply. The hairs of my head, catching terror from my fancies, erected themselves.

Again I advanced, and again I became aware of the sensation of contact. With a quick movement I passed my hand upward and downward.

It was indeed he. He was half-reclining, half-standing against a wall of the chamber: that he was not dead, I at once knew by his uneasy breathing. Indeed, when, having chafed his hands for some time, I tried to rouse him, he quickly recovered himself, and muttered: "I fainted; I want sleep — only sleep." I bore him back to the lighted room, assisted by Ham in the latter part of the journey. Ham's ecstasies were infinite; he had hardly hoped to see his master's face again. His garments being wet and soiled, the negro divested him of them, and dressed him in a tightly-fitting scarlet robe of Babylonish pattern, reaching to the feet, but leaving the lower neck and forearm bare, and girt round the stomach by a broad gold-orphreyed *ceinture*. With all the tenderness of a woman, the man stretched his master thus arrayed on the couch. Here he kept an Argus guard while

Zaleski, in one deep unbroken slumber of a night and a day, reposed before him. When at last the sleeper woke, in his eye — full of divine instinct — flitted the wonted falchion-flash of the whetted, two-edged intellect; the secret, austere, self-conscious smile of triumph curved his lip; not a trace of pain or fatigue remained. After a substantial meal on nuts, autumn fruits, and wine of Samos, he resumed his place on the couch; and I sat by his side to hear the story of his wandering. He said:

"We have, Shiel, had before us a very remarkable series of murders, and a very remarkable series of suicides. Were they in any way connected? To this extent, I think — that the mysterious, the unparalleled nature of the murders gave rise to a morbid condition in the public mind, which in turn resulted in the epidemic of suicide. But though such an epidemic has its origin in the instinct of imitation so common in men, you must not suppose that the mental process is a *conscious* one. A person feels an impulse to go and do *likewise*. He would indeed repudiate such an assumption. Thus one man destroys himself, and another imitates him — but whereas the former uses a pistol, the latter uses a rope. It is rather absurd, therefore, to imagine that in any of those cases in which the slip of papyrus has been found in the mouth after death, the cause of death has been the slavish imitativeness of the suicidal mania — for this, as I say, is never *slavish*. The papyrus then — quite apart from the unmistakable evidences of suicide invariably left by each self-destroyer — affords us definite and certain means by which we can distinguish the two classes of deaths; and we are thus able to divide the total number into two nearly equal halves.

"But you start — you are troubled — you never heard or

read of murder such as this, the simultaneous murder of thousands over wide areas of the face of the globe; here you feel is something outside your experience, deeper than your profoundest imaginings. To the question 'by whom committed?' and 'with what motive?' your mind can conceive no possible answer. And yet the answer must be, 'by man, and for human motives,' — for the Angel of Death with flashing eye and flaming sword is himself long dead; and again we can say at once, by no *one* man, but by many, a cohort, an army of men; and again, by no *common* men, but by men hellish (or heavenly) in cunning, in resource, in strength and unity of purpose; men laughing to scorn the flimsy prophylactics of society, separated by an infinity of self-confidence and spiritual integrity from the ordinary easily-crushed criminal of our days.

"This much at least I was able to discover from the first; and immediately I set myself to the detection of motive by a careful study of each case. This, too, in due time, became clear to me — but to motive it may perhaps be more convenient to refer later on. What next engaged my attention was the figures on the papyrus, and devoutly did I hope that by their solution I might be able to arrive at some more exact knowledge of the mystery.

"The figures round the border first attracted me, and the mere *reading* of them gave me very little trouble. But I was convinced that behind their meaning thus read lay some deep esoteric significance; and this, almost to the last, I was utterly unable to fathom. You perceive that these border figures consist of waved lines of two different lengths, drawings of snakes, triangles looking like the Greek delta, and a heart-shaped object with a dot following it. These succeed one another in a certain definite order on all the slips. What, I asked myself, were these drawings meant to represent — letters, numbers, things, or abstractions? This I was the more readily able to determine because I have often, in thinking over the shape of the Roman letter *S,* wondered whether it did not owe its convolute form to an attempt on the part of its inventor to make a picture of the

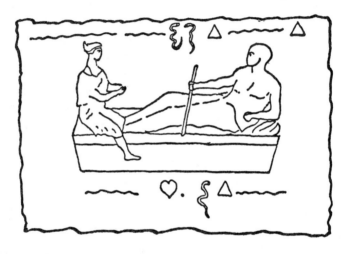

serpent; S being the sibilant or hissing letter, and the serpent the hissing animal. This view, I fancy (though I am not sure), has escaped the philologists, but of course you know that all letters were originally *pictures of things,* and of what was *S* a picture, if not of the serpent? I therefore assumed, by way of trial, that the snakes in the diagram stood for a sibilant letter, that is, either *C* or *S.* And thence, supposing this to be the case, I deduced: firstly, that all the other figures stood for letters; and secondly, that they all appeared in the form of pictures of the things of which those letters were originally meant to be pictures. Thus

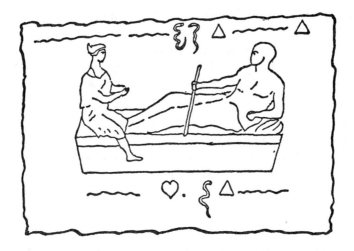

the letter 'm,' one of the four *'liquid'* consonants, is, as we now
write it, only a shortened form of a waved line; and as a waved
line it was originally written, and was the character by which *a
stream of running water* was represented in writing; indeed it
only owes its name to the fact that when the lips are pressed
together, and 'm' uttered by a continuous effort, a certain
resemblance to the murmur of running water is produced. The
longer waved line in the diagram I therefore took to represent
'm'; and it at once followed that the shorter meant 'n,' for no
two letters of the commoner European alphabets differ *only* in
length (as distinct from shape) except 'm' and 'n,' and 'w' and
'v'; indeed, just as the French call 'w' 'double-ve,' so very
properly might 'm' be called 'double-en.' But, in this case, the
longer not being 'w,' the shorter could not be 'v': it was
therefore 'n.' And now there only remained the heart and the
triangle. I was unable to think of any letter that could ever have

been intended for the picture of a heart, but the triangle I knew to be the letter *A*. This was originally written without the cross-bar from prop to prop, and the two feet at the bottom of the props were not separated as now, but joined; so that the letter formed a true triangle. It was meant by the primitive man to be a picture of his primitive house, this house being, of course, hut-shaped, and consisting of a conical roof without walls. I had thus, with the exception of the heart, disentangled the whole, which then (leaving a space for the heart) read as follows:

'mn $\left\{ \begin{array}{l} \text{ss} \\ \text{cc} \end{array} \right.$ anan . . . san.'

"But 'c' before 'a' being never a sibilant (except in some few so-called 'Romance' languages), but a guttural, it was for the

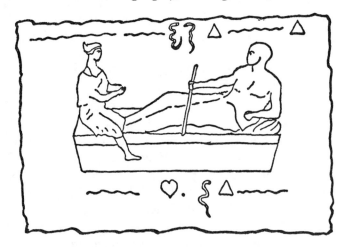

moment discarded; also as no word begins with the letters 'mn' — except 'mnemonics' and its fellows — I concluded that a vowel must be omitted between these letters, and thence that all vowels (except 'a') were omitted; again, as the double 's' can never come after 'n' I saw that either a vowel was omitted between the two 's's,' or that the first word ended after the first 's.' Thus I got

'm ns sanan . . . san,'

or, supplying the now quite obvious vowels,

'mens sana in . . . sano.'

"The heart I now knew represented the word 'corpore,' the Latin word for 'heart' being 'cor,' and the dot — showing that the word as it stood was an abbreviation — conclusively proved every one of my deductions.

"So far all had gone flowingly. It was only when I came to consider the central figures that for many days I spent my strength in vain. You heard my exclamation of delight and astonishment when at last a ray of light pierced the gloom. At no time, indeed, was I wholly in the dark as to the *general* significance of these figures, for I saw at once their resemblance to the sepulchral reliefs of classical times. In case you are not minutely acquainted with the technique of these stones, I may as well show you one, which I myself removed from an old grave in Tarentum."

He took from a niche a small piece of close-grained marble, about a foot square, and laid it before me. On one side it was exquisitely sculptured in relief.

"This," he continued, "is a typical example of the Greek grave-stone, and having seen one specimen you may be said to have seen almost all, for there is surprisingly little variety in the class. You will observe that the scene represents a man reclining on a couch; in his hand he holds a *patera,* or dish, filled with grapes and pomegranates, and beside him is a tripod bearing the viands from which he is banqueting. At his feet sits a woman — for the Greek lady never reclined at table. In addition to these two figures a horse's head, a dog, or a serpent may sometimes be seen; and these forms comprise the almost invariable pattern of all grave reliefs. Now, that this was the real model from which the figures on the papyrus were taken I could not doubt, when I considered the seemingly absurd fidelity with which in each murder the papyrus, smeared with honey, was placed under the tongue of the victim. I said to myself: it can only be that the assassins have bound themselves to the observance of a strict and narrow ritual from which no departure is under any circumstances permitted — perhaps for the sake of signalling the course of events to others at a distance. But what ritual? That question I was able to answer when I knew the answer to these others — why *under the tongue,* and why *smeared with honey?* For no reason, except that the Greeks (not the Romans till very late in their history) always placed an *obolos,* or penny, beneath the tongue of the dead to pay his passage across the Stygian river of ghosts; for no reason, except that to these same Greeks honey was a sacred fluid, intimately associated in their minds with the mournful subject of Death; a fluid with which the bodies of the deceased were anointed, and sometimes — especially in Sparta and the Pelasgic South — embalmed; with which libations were poured to Hermes Psuchopompos, conductor of the dead to the regions of shade; with which offerings were made to all the chthonic deities, and the souls of the departed in general. You remember, for instance, the melancholy words of Helen addressed to Hermione in *Orestes:*

Καὶ λαβὲ χοὰς τάσδ' ἐν χεροῖν κόμας τ' εμὰς. ἐλθοῦσα
δ' ἀμφὶ τὸν Κλυταιμνήστρας τάφον μελίκρατ' ἄφες
γάλακτος οἰνωπόν τ' ἄχνην.

"And so everywhere. The ritual then of the murderers was a *Greek* ritual, their cult a Greek cult — preferably, perhaps, a South Greek one, a Spartan one, for it was here that the highly conservative peoples of that region clung longest and fondliest to this semi-barbarous worship. This then being so, I was made all the more certain of my conjecture that the central figures on the papyrus were drawn from a Greek model.

"Here, however, I came to a standstill. I was infinitely puzzled by the rod in the man's hand. In none of the Greek grave-reliefs does any such thing as a rod make an appearance, except in one well-known example where the god Hermes — generally represented as carrying the *caduceus,* or staff, given him by Phoebus — appears leading a dead maiden to the land of night. But in every other example of which I am aware the sculpture represents a man *living,* not dead, banqueting *on earth,* not in Hades, by the side of his living companion. What then could be the significance of the staff in the hand of this living man? It was only after days of the hardest struggle, the cruellest suspense, that the thought flashed on me that the idea of Hermes leading away the dead female might, in this case, have been carried one step farther; that the male figure might be no living man, no man at all, but *Hermes himself* actually banqueting in Hades with the soul of his disembodied *protégée!* The thought filled me with a rapture I cannot describe, and you witnessed my excitement. But, at all events, I saw that this was a truly tremendous departure from Greek art and thought, to which in general the copyists seemed to cling so religiously. There must therefore be a reason, a strong reason, for vandalism such as this. And that, at any rate, it was no longer difficult to discover; for now I knew that the male figure was no mortal, but a god, a spirit, a DAEMON (in the Greek sense of the word); and the female figure I saw by the marked shortness of her drapery to be no Athenian, but a Spartan; no matron either, but a maiden, a lass, a LASSIE; and now I had forced on me lassie daemon, *Lacedaemon.*

"This then was the badge, the so carefully-buried badge, of this society of men. The only thing which still puzzled and confounded me at this stage was the startling circumstance that a *Greek* society should make use of a *Latin* motto. It was clear that either all my conclusions were totally wrong, or else the motto *mens sana in corpore sano* contained wrapped up in itself some acroamatic meaning which I found myself unable to penetrate, and which the authors had found no Greek motto capable of conveying. But at any rate, having found this much, my knowledge led me of itself one step further; for I perceived that, widely extended as were their operations, the society was necessarily in the main an *English,* or at least an English-speaking one — for of this the word 'lassie' was plainly indicative: it was easy now to conjecture London, the monster-city in which all things lose themselves, as their headquarters; and at this point in my investigations I despatched to the papers the advertisement you have seen."

"But," I exclaimed, "even now I utterly fail to see by what mysterious processes of thought you arrived at the wording of the advertisement; even now it conveys no meaning to my mind.''

''That,'' he replied, ''will grow clear when we come to a right understanding of the baleful *motive* which inspired these men. I have already said that I was not long in discovering it. There was only one possible method of doing so — and that was, by all means, by any means, to find out some condition or other common to every one of the victims before death. It is true that I was unable to do this in some few cases, but where I failed, I was convinced that my failure was due to the insufficiency of the evidence at my disposal, rather than to the actual absence of the condition. Now, let us take almost any two cases you will, and seek for this common condition: let us take, for example, the first two that attracted the attention of the world — the poor woman of the slums of Berlin, and the celebrated man of science. Separated by as wide an interval as they are, we shall yet find, if we look closely, in each case the same pathetic tokens of the still unelimination *striae* of our poor humanity. The woman is not an old woman, for she has a 'small young' family, which, had she lived, might have been increased: notwithstanding which, she has suffered from hemiplegia, 'partial paralysis.' The professor, too, has had not one, but two, large families, and an 'army of grandchildren': but note well the startling, the hideous fact, that *every one of his children is dead!* The crude grave has gaped before the cock to suck in *every one* of those shrunk forms, so indigent of vital impulse, so pauper of civism, lust, so drafty, so vague, so lean — but not before they have had time to dower with the ah and woe of their infirmity a whole wretched 'army of grandchildren.' And yet this man of wisdom is on the point, in his old age, of marrying once again, of producing for the good of his race still more of this poor human stuff. You see the lurid significance, the point of resemblance — you see it? And, O heaven, is it not too sad? For me, I tell you, the whole business has a tragic pitifulness too deep for words. But this brings me to the discussion of a large matter. It would, for instance, be interesting to me to hear what you, a modern European, saturated with all the notions of your little day, what *you* consider the supreme, the all-important question for the nations of Europe at this moment. Am I far wrong in assuming that you would rattle off half a dozen of the moot points agitating rival factions in your own land, select one of them, and call that 'the question of the hour'? I wish I could see as you see; I wish to God I did not see deeper. In order to lead you to my point, what, let me ask you, what *precisely* was it that ruined the old nations — that brought, say Rome, to her knees at last? Centralization, you say, top-heavy imperialism, dilettante pessimism, the love of luxury. At bottom, believe me, it was not one of these high-sounding things — it was simply war; the sum total of the battles of centuries. But let me explain myself: this is a novel view to you, and you are perhaps unable to conceive how or why war was so fatal to the old world, because you see how little harmful it is to the new. If you collected in a promiscuous way a few millions of modern Englishmen and slew them all simultaneously, what, think you, would be the effect from the point of view of the State? The effect, I conceive, would be indefinitely small, wonderfully transitory; there would, of course, be a momentary lacuna in the boiling surge: yet the womb of humanity is full of sap, and uberant; Ocean-tide, wooed of that Ilithyia whose breasts are many, would flow on, and the void would soon be filled. But the effect would only be thus insignificant, if, as I said, your millions were taken promiscuously (as in the modern army), not if they were *picked* men —— in *that* case the loss (or gain) would be excessive, and permanent for all time. Now, the war-hosts of the ancient commonwealths — not dependent on the mechanical contrivances of the modern army — were necessarily composed of the very best men: the strong-boned, the heart-stout, the sound in wind and limb. Under these conditions the State shuddered through all her frame, thrilled adown every filament, at the death of a single one of her sons in the field. As only the feeble, the aged, bided at home, their number after each battle became larger *in proportion to the whole* than before. Thus the nation, more and more, with ever-increasing rapidity, declined in bodily, and of course spiritual, quality, until the *end* was reached, and Nature swallowed up the weaklings whole; and thus war, which to the modern state is at worst the blockhead and indecent *affaires d'honneur* of persons in office — and which, surely, before you and I die will cease altogether — was to the ancient a genuine and remorselessly fatal scourge.

"And now let me apply these facts to the Europe of our own time. We no longer have world-serious war — but in its place we have a scourge, the effect of which on the modern state is *precisely the same* as the effect of war on the ancient, only — in the end — far more destructive, far more subtle, sure, horrible, disgusting. The name of this pestilence is Medical Science. Yes, it is most true, shudder — shudder — as you will! Man's best friend turns to an asp in his bosom to sting him to the basest of deaths. The devastating growth of medical, and especially surgical, science — that, if you like, for us all, is 'the question of the hour'! And what a question! of what surpassing importance, in the presence of which all other 'questions' whatever dwindle into mere academic triviality. For just as the ancient State was wounded to the heart through the death of her healthy sons in the field, just so slowly, just so silently, is the modern receiving deadly hurt by the botching and tinkering of her unhealthy children. The net result is in each case the same — the altered ratio of the total amount of reproductive health to the total amount of reproductive disease. They recklessly spent their best; we sedulously conserve our worst; and as they pined and died of anaemia, so we, unless we repent, must perish in a paroxysm of black-blood apoplexy. And this prospect becomes more certain, when you reflect that the physician as we know him is not, like other men and things, a being of gradual growth, of slow evolution: from Adam to the middle of the last century the world saw nothing even in the least resembling him. No son of Paian *he,* but a fatherless, full-grown birth from the incessant matrix of Modern Time, so motherly of monstrous litters of 'Gorgon and Hydra and Chimaeras dire'; you will understand what I mean when you consider the quite recent date of, say, the introduction of anaesthetics or antiseptics, the discovery of the knee-jerk, bacteriology, or even of such a doctrine as the circulation of the blood. We are at this very time, if I mistake not, on the verge of new insights which will enable man to laugh at disease — laugh at it in the sense of overruling its natural tendency to produce death, not by any means in the sense of destroying its ever-expanding *existence.* Do you know that at this moment your hospitals are crammed with beings in human likeness suffering from a thousand obscure and subtly-ineradicable ills, all of whom, if left alone, would die almost at once, but ninety in the hundred of whom will, as it is, be sent forth 'cured,' like missionaries of hell, and the horrent shapes of Night and Acheron, to mingle in the pure river of humanity the poison-taint of their protean vileness? Do you know that in your schools one-quarter of the children are already purblind? Have you gauged the importance of your tremendous consumption of quack catholicons, of the fortunes derived from their sale, of the spread of modern nervous disorders, of toothless youth and thrice loathsome age among the helot-classes? Do you know that in the course of my late journey to London, I walked from Piccadilly Circus to Hyde Park Corner, during which time I observed some five hundred people, of whom twenty-seven only were perfectly healthy, well-formed men, and eighteen healthy, beautiful women? On every hand — with a thrill of intensest joy, I say it! — is to be seen, if not yet commencing civilization, then progress, progress — wide as the world — toward it: only here — at the heart — is there decadence, fatty degeneration. Brain-evolution — and favoring airs — and the ripening time — and the silent Will of God, of God — all these in conspiracy seem to be behind, urging the whole ship's company of us to some undreamable luxury of glory — when lo, this check, artificial, evitable. Less death, more disease — that is the sad, the unnatural record; children especially — so sensitive to the physician's art — living on by hundreds of thousands, bearing within them the germs of wide-spreading sorrow, who in former times would have died. And if you consider that the proper function of the doctor is the strictly limited one of curing the curable, rather than of self-gloriously perpetuating the incurable, you may find it difficult to give a quite rational answer to this simple question: *why?* Nothing is so sure as that to the unit it is a cruelty; nothing so certain as that to humanity it is a wrong;

to say that such and such a one was sent by the All Wise, and must *therefore* be not merely permitted, but elaborately coaxed and forced, to live, is to utter a blasphemy against Man at which even the ribald tongue of a priest might falter; and as a matter of fact, society, in just contempt for this species of argument, never hesitates to hang, for its own imagined good, its heaven-sent catholics, protestants, sheep, sheep-stealers, etc. What then, you ask, would I do with these unholy ones? To save the State would I pierce them with a sword, or leave them to the slow throes of their agonies? Ah, do not expect me to answer that question — I do not know what to answer. The whole spirit of the present is one of a broad and beautiful, if quite thoughtless, humanism, and I, a child of the present, cannot but be borne along by it, coerced into sympathy with it. 'Beautiful' I say: for if anywhere in the world you have seen a sight more beautiful than a group of hospital *savants* bending with endless scrupulousness over a little pauper child, concentering upon its frailty the whole human skill and wisdom of ages, so have not I. Here have you the full realization of a parable diviner than that of the man who went down from Jerusalem to Jericho. Beautiful then; with at least surface beauty, like the serpent *lachesis mutus;* but, like many beautiful things, deadly too, *in*human. And, on the whole, an answer will have to be found. As for me, it is a doubt which has often agitated me, whether the central dogma of Judaism and Christianity alike can, after all, be really one of the inner verities of this our earthly being — the dogma, that by the shedding of the innocent blood, and by that alone, shall the race of man find cleansing and salvation. Will no agony of reluctance overcome the necessity that one man die, 'so that the whole people perish not'? Can it be true that by nothing less than the 'three days of pestilence' shall the land be purged of its stain, and is this old divine alternative about to confront us in new, modern form? Does the inscrutable Artemis indeed demand offerings of human blood to suage her anger? Most sad that man should ever need, should ever have needed, to foul his hand in the μυσαρὸν αἷμα of his own veins! But what is, is. And can it be fated that the most advanced civilization of the future shall needs have in it, as the first and chief element of its glory, the most barbarous of all the rituals of barbarism — the immolation of hecatombs which wail a muling human wail? Is it indeed part of man's strange destiny through the deeps of Time that he one day bow his back to the duty of pruning himself as a garden, so that he run not to a waste wilderness? Shall the physician, the *accoucheur,* of the time to come be expected, and commanded, to do on the ephod and breast-plate, anoint his head with the oil of gladness, and add to the function of healer the function of Sacrificial Priest? These you say, are wild, dark questions. Wild enough, dark enough. We know how Sparta — the 'man-taming Sparta' Simonides calls her — answered them. Here was the complete subordination of all unit-life to the well-being of the Whole. The child, immediately on his entry into the world, fell under the control of the State: it was not left to the judgment of his parents, as elsewhere, whether he should be brought up or not, but a commission of the Phyle in which he was born decided the question. If he was weakly, if he had any bodily unsightliness, he was exposed on a place called Taygetus, and so perished. It was a consequence of this that never did the sun in his course light on man half so godly stalwart, on woman half so houri-lovely, as in stern and stout old Sparta. Death, like all mortal, they must bear; disease, once and for all, they were resolved to have done with. The word which they used to express the idea 'ugly,' meant also 'hateful,' 'vile,' 'disgraceful' — and I need hardly point out to you the significance of that fact alone; for they considered — and rightly — that there is no sort of natural reason why every denizen of earth should not be perfectly hale, integral, sane, beautiful — if only very moderate pains be taken to procure this divine result. One fellow, indeed, called Nancleidas, grew a little too fat to please the sensitive eyes of the Spartans: I believe he was periodically whipped. Under a system so very barbarous, the super-sweet, egoistic voice of the club-footed poet Byron would, of course, never have been heard: one brief egoistic 'lament' on Taygetus, and so an end. It is not, however, certain that the world could not have managed very well without Lord Byron. The one thing that admits of no contradiction is that it cannot manage without the holy citizen, and that disease, to men and to nations, can have but one meaning, annihilation near or ultimate. At any rate, from these remarks, you will now very likely be able to arrive at some understanding of the wording of the advertisements which I sent to the papers.''

Zaleski, having delivered himself of this singular *tirade,* paused: replaced the sepulchral relief in its niche: drew a drapery of silver cloth over his bare feet and the hem of his antique garment of Babylon: and then continued:

''After some time the answer to the advertisement at length arrived; but what was my disgust to find that it was perfectly unintelligible to me. I had asked for a date and an address: the reply came giving a date, and an address, too — but an address wrapped up in cypher, which, of course, I, as a supposed member of the society, was expected to be able to read. At any rate, I now knew the significance of the incongruous circumstance that the Latin proverb *mens sana etc.* should be adopted as the motto of a Greek society; the significance lay in this, that the motto *contained an address* — the address of their meeting-place, or at least, or their chief meeting-place. I was now confronted with the task of solving — and of solving quickly, without the loss of an hour — this enigma; and I confess that it was only by the most violent and extraordinary concentration of what I may call the dissecting faculty, that I was able to do so in good time. And yet there was no special difficulty in the matter. For looking at the motto as it stood in cypher, the first thing I perceived was that, in order to read the secret, the heart-shaped figure must be left out of consideration, if there was any *consistency* in the system of cyphers at all, for it belonged to a class of symbols quite distinct from that of all the others, not being, like them, a picture-letter. Omitting this, therefore, and taking all the other vowels and consonants whether actually represented in the device or not, I now got the proverb in the form *mens sana in . . . pore sano.* I wrote this down, and what instantly struck me was the immense, the altogether unusual, number of *liquids* in the motto — six in all, amounting to no less than one-third of the total number of letters! Putting these all together you get *mnnn-nr,* and you can see that the very appearance of the 'm's' and 'n's' (especially when *written*) running into one another, of it-self suggests a stream of water. Having previously arrived at the conclusion of London as the meeting-place, I could not now fail to go on to the inference of *the Thames;* there, or near there, would I find those whom I sought. The letters 'mnnnnr,' then, meant the Thames: what did the still remaining letters mean? I now took these remaining letters, placing them side by side: I got aaa, sss, ee, oo, p, and i. Juxtaposing these nearly in the order indicated by the frequency of their occurrence, and their place in the Roman alphabet, you at once and inevitably get the word *AEsopi*. And now I was fairly startled by this symmetrical proof of the exactness of my own deductions in other respects, but, above all, far above all, by the occurrence of that word *'AEsopi.'* For who was AEsopus? He was a slave who was freed for his wise and witful sallies: he is therefore typical of the liberty of the wise — their moral manumission from temporary and narrow law; he was also a close friend of Croesus: he is typical, then, of the union of wisdom with wealth — true wisdom with real wealth, lastly, and above all, he was thrown by the Delphians from a rock on account of his wit: he is typical, therefore, of death — the shedding of blood — as a result of wisdom, this thought being an elaboration of Solomon's great maxim, 'in much wisdom is much sorrow.' But how accurately all this fitted in with what would naturally be the doctrines of the men on whose track I was! I could no longer doubt the justness of my reasonings, and immediately, while you slept, I set off for London.

"Of my haps in London I need not give you a very particular account. The meeting was to be held on the fifteenth, and by the morning of the thirteenth I had reached a place called Wargrave, on the Thames. There I hired a light canoe, and thence proceeded down the river in a somewhat zig-zag manner, narrowly examining the banks on either side, and keeping a sharp out-look for some board, or sign, or house, that would seem to betoken any sort of connection with the word 'AEsopi.' In this way I passed a fruitless day, and having reached the shipping region, made fast my craft, and in a spirit of *diablerie* spent the night in a common lodging-house, in the company of the most remarkable human beings, characterized by an odor of alcohol, and a certain obtrusive *bonne camaraderie* which the prevailing fear of death could not altogether repress. By dawn of the fourteenth I was on my journey again — on, and ever on. Eagerly I longed for a sight of the word I sought: but I had misjudged the men against whose cunning I had measured my own. I should have remembered more consistently that they were no ordinary men. As I was destined to find, there lay a deeper more cabalistic meaning in the motto than any I had been able to dream of. I had proceeded on my pilgrimage down the river a long way past Greenwich, and had now reached a desolate and level reach of land stretching away on either hand. Paddling my boat from the right to the left bank, I came to a spot where a little arm of the river ran up some few yards into the land. The place wore a specially dreary and deserted aspect: the land was flat, and covered with low shrubs. I rowed into this arm of shallow water and rested on my oar, wearily bethinking myself what was next to be done. Looking round, however, I saw to my surprise that at the end of this arm there was a short narrow pathway — a winding road — leading from the riverbank. I stood up in the boat and followed its course with my eyes. It was met by another road also winding among the bushes, but in a slightly different direction. At the end of this was a little, low, high-roofed, round house, without doors or windows. And then — and then — tingling now with a thousand raptures — I beheld a pool of water near this structure, and then another low house, a counterpart of the first — and then, still leading on in the same direction, another pool — and then a great rock, heart-shaped —

and then another winding road — and then another pool of water. All was a model — *exact to the minutest particular* — of the device on the papyrus! The first long-waved line was the river itself; the three short-waved lines were the arm of the river and the two pools; the three snakes were the three winding roads; the two triangles representing the letter *A* were the two

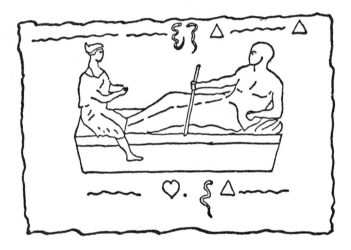

high-roofed round houses; the heart was the rock! I sprang, now thoroughly excited, from the boat, and ran in headlong haste to the end of the last lake. Here there was a rather thick and high growth of bushes, but peering among them, my eye at once caught a white oblong board supported on a stake: on this, in black letters, was marked the words, 'Descensus Æsopi.' It was necessary, therefore, to go *down:* the meeting-place was sub-terranean. It was without difficulty that I discovered a small opening in the ground, half-hidden by the underwood; from the orifice I found that a series of wooden steps led directly downwards, and I at once boldly descended. No sooner, however, had I touched the bottom than I was confronted by an ancient man in Hellenic apparel, armed with the Greek *ziphos* and *peltè*. His eyes, accustomed to the gloom, pierced me long with an earnest scrutiny.

" 'You are a Spartan?' he asked at length.

" 'Yes,' I answered promptly.

" 'Then how is it you do not know that I am stone deaf?'

"I shrugged, indicating that for the moment I had forgotten the fact.

" 'You *are* a Spartan?' he repeated.

"I nodded with emphasis.

" 'Then, how is it you omit to make the sign?'

"Now, you must not suppose that at this point I was nonplussed, for in that case you would not give due weight to the strange inherent power of the mind to rise to the occasion of a sudden emergency — to stretch itself long to the length of an event; I do not hesitate to say that *no* combination of circumstances can defeat a vigorous brain fully alert, and in possession of itself. With a quickness to which the lightning-flash is tardy, I remembered that this was a spot indicated by the symbols on the papyrus: I remembered that this same papyrus was always placed under the *tongue* of the dead; I remembered, too, that among that very nation whose language had afforded the motto, to 'turn up the *thumb*' (*pollicem vertere*) was a symbol significant of death. I touched the under surface of my tongue with the tip of my thumb. The aged man was appeased. I passed on, and examined the place.

"It was simply a vast circular hall, the arched roof of which was supported on colonnades of what I took to be pillars of porphyry. Down the middle and round the sides ran tables of the same material; the walls were clothed in hangings of sable velvet, on which, in infinite reproduction, was embroidered in cypher the motto of the society. The chairs were cushioned in the same stuff. Near the center of the circle stood a huge statue of what really seemed to me to be pure beaten gold. On the great ebon base was inscribed the word ΛΥΚΥΡΓΟΣ. From the roof swung by brazen chains a single misty lamp.

"Having seen this much I reascended to the land of light, and being fully resolved on attending the meeting on the next day or night, and not knowing what my fate might then be, I wrote to inform you of the means by which my body might be traced.

"But on the next day a new thought occurred to me: I reasoned thus: 'these men are not common assassins; they wage a too rash warfare against diseased life, but not against life in general. In all probability they have a quite immoderate, quite morbid reverence for the sanctity of healthy life. They will not therefore take mine, *unless* they suppose me to be the only living outsider who has a knowledge of their secret, and therefore think it absolutely necessary for the carrying out of their beneficent designs that my life should be sacrificed. I will therefore prevent such a motive from occurring to them by communicating to another their whole secret, and — if the necessity should arise — *letting them know* that I have done so, without telling them who that other is. Thus my life will be assured.' I therefore wrote to you on that day a full account of all I had discovered, giving you to understand, however, on the envelope, that you need not examine the contents for some little time.

"I waited in the subterranean vault during the greater part of the next day; but not till midnight did the confederates gather. What happened at that meeting I shall not disclose, even to you. All was sacred — solemn — full of awe. Of the choral hymns there sung, the hierophantic ritual, liturgies, paeans, the gorgeous symbolisms — of the wealth there represented, the culture, art, self-sacrifice — of the mingling of all the tongues of Europe — I shall not speak; nor shall I repeat names which you would at once recognize as familiar to you — though I may, perhaps, mention that the 'Morris,' whose name appears on the papyrus sent to me is a well-known *littérateur* of that name. But this in confidence, for some years at least.

"Let me, however, hurry to a conclusion. My turn came to speak. I rose undaunted, and calmly disclosed myself; during the moment of hush, of wide-eyed paralysis that ensued, I declared that fully as I coincided with their views in general, I found myself unable to regard their methods with approval — these I could not but consider too rash, too harsh, too premature. My voice was suddenly drowned by one universal, earth-shaking roar of rage and contempt, during which I was surrounded on all sides, seized, pinioned, and dashed on the central table. All this time, in the hope and love of life, I passionately shouted that I was not the only living being who shared in their secret. But my voice was drowned, and drowned again, in the whirling tumult. None heard me. A powerful and little-known anaesthetic — the means by which all their murders have been accomplished — was now produced. A cloth, saturated with the fluid, was placed on my mouth and nostrils. I was stifled. Sense failed. The incubus of the universe blackened down upon my brain. How I tugged at the mandrakes of speech! was a locked pugilist with language! In the depth of my extremity the half-thought, I remember, floated, like a mist, through my fading consciousness, that now perhaps — now — there was silence around me; that *now,* could my palsied lips find dialect, I should be heard, and understood. My whole soul rose focussed to the effort — my body jerked itself upwards. At that moment I knew my spirit truly great, genuinely sublime. For I *did* utter something — my dead and shuddering tongue *did* babble forth some coherency. Then I fell back, and all was once more the ancient Dark. On the next day when I woke, I was lying on my back in my little boat, placed there by God knows whose hands. At all events, one thing was clear — I *had* uttered something — I was saved. With what of strength remained to me I reached the place where I had left your *calèche,* and started on my homeward way. The necessity to sleep was strong upon me, for the fumes of the anaesthetic still clung about my brain; hence, after my long journey, I fainted on my passage through the house, and in this condition you found me.

"Such then is the history of my thinkings and doings in connection with this ill-advised confraternity: and now that their cabala is known to others — to how many others *they* cannot guess — I think it is not unlikely that we shall hear little more of the Society of Sparta."

The Return of Prince Zaleski

The mist dribbled a little drizzle in bitter mood as the Murena funeral moved through a London that turned up coat collars in response to that October blur. To Captain Campos of the Spanish Embassy, who was with me in my cab, I remarked, "All these people going about their little businesses have in them the same one care — an apprehension of death, a sense of *I may be the next.*"

"Of a certainty," my diplomat friend answered, "evil is in the air — corruption like the offensive breath of vampires, and ghouls, and bats of darkness, that foully suck the blood of carcasses. This killing of Murena is the thirteenth within a month, and the seventh murder of a Spaniard."

"Inefficiency of the police!" I said. "Moreover, I think, in every case — your seven Spaniards and our six Londoners — the monster has left a note with his victim — as if the murderer were challenging us to catch him."

"Say, Señor Shiel," Campos suddenly said, "why should *you* not intervene? It is Inspector Chamberlain's suggestion to us that you approach your friend, Prince Zaleski, and ask his help."

"Well, well," I answered, "but then Zaleski, you understand, is a man who has deliberately elected to live a hermit existence. No man sees his face but his Nubian servant, Ham, who keeps his organ's wind-chests going and cooks his porridge.

His address is a Monmouthshire abbey — mainly a ruin, Zaleski and Ham being its hermit monks. Still, I will think of it.''

And I did. After watching that wounded body of Juan Murena lowered into its solitary crib, I wrote to Prince Zaleski, who presently sent me a ''Come'' of invitation; and, not without peril, I clambered over broken stone in a growing gloom to that apartment on high that was my anchorite's habitat, whereupon Zaleski sprang to welcome me in his brisk way, saying: ''The very face I craved to see! You know, my friend, how Newton assumed that the velocity of light is infinite, and all we like geese have gone agabbling after. I have been thinking. . . . You will now pull my semantic reactions into harmony with the facts, and make of me an intellect clean-shaven.''

''I have come on a practical matter,'' I mentioned.

And he: ''I *know* what you have come on; for my Ham, who reads 'the papers,' has told me of what is now rousing the outside world to commotion. But you will hardly, I think, find me eager to pit my wits against the lady's, who without doubt is an egregious priestess of outrage.''

''Lady!'' I exclaimed. ''You say to me, Zaleski, that these demoniacal crimes are being committed by a woman?''

He answered, ''Are they not womanly crimes? Half of them, anyway. There is a certain needless world-challenge, self-assertiveness, which is female. She even dares to publish her address.''

Where did she dare? When? But now in came Ham, bearing trays, and we sat under the moonshine of a hanging *lampas* to one of Zaleski's repasts. That night long we talked of velocities, of space-time, entropy, and of Newton's *hypotheses non fingo* — of anything, in fact, but what was really interesting me.

It was the following afternoon before I could broach my subject again; when I said to Zaleski: "But, after all, in respect to those atrocities, it is a question of rescuing yet other lives from atrocity, so that the notion of duty comes in."

"Let it be so, then," he answered. "The relation between the woman, or her wraith, and me, and between her wraith and Ham, is nearer than you know — whatever species of thing a 'wraith' may be. Certainly she is dreadful, and I have a dread of her, as I frankly said to one Chamberlain of the police when he succeeded in coming here. But you, Shiel, tell me the facts as you know them; perhaps we two will see some way out."

Whereupon I spent two hours of telling, with Zaleski reclining, smoking a narghile, his eyes shut, save when he sat sharply up with increasing interest. I began at the end with visiting Juan Murena, Press Secretary of the new Spanish King. Murena was in a waltzing mood that night at his Embassy's ball; he was talking in the ballroom with a group (two of the group being friends of mine), and he led the talk, his theme being the New Spain, as it often was, claiming Spain would be a World Power again and was romping straight to own an Empire such as it never before had owned. "I at least," he declared, "mean to live to see it." But he did not; just then a message came to him to say that somebody in the Code Writer's Room was waiting to see him, and thither Murena's doomed feet took him. That "somebody" was later said to be "a young man in an opera cloak." Whoever he was, there in that Code Writer's Room the patriotic Murena was found butchered, ghastly, his throat gashed, and in his grasp a scrap of paper scribbled on, as in all previous cases.

A reproduction of this scrap, taken from an article in *The*

Times commenting on the crime, I handed to Zaleski. The scrap, as reproduced, read as follows:

"You would learn its meaning, Shiel?" Zaleski laid the newspaper clipping between us upon a small inlaid table of Algerian workmanship. "It is quite simple. Here we have a mother and a son, the son an adorer of the mother, who thinks it well to mystify the *investigating heads* who in turn have the fixed idea that the murders are all perpetrated by one person — to mystify those heads by embarrassing that fixed idea of theirs with a new concept that the murders may possibly have been done by two persons. Those *heads* are now certain to revert with even more fixity to the conviction that the perpetrator is one person — now certain to conclude that two is an untrue ruse of the perpetrator to disburden himself of half his criminality. It is rather a deep move of the mother; she even gives her address in cypher. The son, it appears, does not quite like giving an address; but then, in giving it, as in everything, he is acting under her direction. However, the reporter of *The Times* catches no glimpse of this giving of an address for the reason that his intellect is all occupied with the idea that the writer of the note was scribbling about a *moth,* whereas he was scribbling about a *Mother* — just the capital *M* alone should prove that Mother was meant, not moth. And the *her* of the script! It is not, as a matter of fact, the female moth that has the *daring* to *dash* itself into the *penetrating heat* (the reporter thinks *hea* to mean *heat*) of a candle's flame! It appears that the female moth emits a luminosity to tempt the male's mentation, as the female glowworm does, so that when the male catches sight of a light of Man, he thinks within himself, 'Here, by Heaven, is femininity!' and perniciously dashes himself to a flaming death. So, if moth was really meant in the script, not *her* but *him* should have been written! Nor is it as to moth and Mother alone that we have confusion in the reporter's *investigating head:* for, space being scanty in the scrap of paper, when the writer was near the end of some lines he made an estimate, in a dim light, as to whether he could get the next word in on that line, and ventured; but in three cases he failed to get the whole word in, so left out a last letter, or two, of the word. Hence in the reproduction of the note we have the syncopations *Moth, hea,* and *len,* the reporter thinking that the writer meant *moth, heat,* and *lent,* the whole for the reporter reading:

My sting to the plotters. And you, investigating heads, leave off investigating. You think me *weak* enough to be netted by you? But the Moth is wise and wary, though venturesome to the *point* of challenging the penetrating heat, even dashing into showing the daring *lent* her, daring to say, 'Here I am,' showing her disdainful audacity.

Then follows the curious geometric drawing, like a signature, giving her address and, I think, her name. But to read *heat* for *hea* can only be due to a preoccupation with the conviction that *Moth* means, not mother, but moth: for *hea* we should read, I easily see, not *heat,* but *head,* since we already have *investigating heads* to guide us, nor can the heat of a candle's flame be described as *penetrating.* As for *len,* to read *lent* seems to me merely feeble. Shakespeare wrote 'The heavens such grace did lend her,' but why did the heavens lend? Why not give? Shakespeare wrote 'lend' simply because 'lend' happens to rhyme with commend. But to make *len* mean *lent,* the reporter actually assumes and adds a comma after *her* —a comma which is not in the reproduction of the note — ignoring that a lens is in the drawing of the signature. So for *len* I read, not *lent,* but *lens,* and I get for the whole note as follows:

My sting to the plotters. And you, investigating heads, leave off investigating. You think me *weak* enough to be netted by you? But the Mother is wise and wary, though venturesome to the *point* of challenging the penetrating head, even dashing into showing the daring *lens,* her daring to say, 'Here I am,' showing her disdainful audacity.

As to the signature, that is clearly the drawing of a double-convex lens having three parallel rays striking upon it, these meeting, as usual, at the principal focus of the lens. If the signature is in fact an address, these three rays can only be three streets, as the two curved sides of the lens can only be crescents; and the fact that the middle line is not continued through the center of the lens demonstrates that the drawing is not of a lens of glass or of light-rays, but depicts a system of streets. Moreover, certain words in the script are underlined, where the underlining is senseless, unless it means to emphasize a pun or double-meaning that indicates name and address: *weak* (or week), for instance, is underlined; *point* is underlined; *len* is underlined; and since *Here I am* means the writer's address, and since the number seven is associated with week, I read the hidden message of the signature as 'Mrs. Point, or Pointer, Number 7 Lens Street, or, more likely, Lens Crescent.'"

"But," I exclaimed, "that is the address of my friend, Lady Poynting — 7 Lens Crescent!"

"Ah?" said Zaleski, quiet satisfaction in his tone.

"Yes, widow of the Marquess of Markstow, a former Ambassador to Madrid, and then widow of Sir Peter Poynting, who was her first husband's attaché. She is a Spaniard, passionate and artistic, and every fourth Sunday she holds a reception that Society scrambles to attend. And yes! — she has a son, Carlos, by her first husband. He is the present Marquess of Markstow."

Zaleski, his eyes closed, now musingly said, "I divine, I know her; for in some species of reverie six midnights ago I somehow experienced the visit of the apparition of a lady, and — in some way or other — I received the impression that this lady and I were destined to come into a mortal combat of wits. I wonder . . . it may have been no more than fancy, but I think that this Lady Poynting is overpatriotic."

"Well, hardly," I answered; "and yet I do not know, for the lady is undoubtedly strange. One Sunday I was the first of her guests to arrive and on approaching the chair in which she was seated, expected some species of greeting from her; but none came; and I had no idea that she might be asleep, for her eyes were open; but then she breathed audibly, like a person who is asleep, though staring at me."

And Zaleski: "Abnormal, you see. What is she like, this lady?"

"Forty-five to fifty years old, tall, thin, colorless, dry as chips, some little faded hairs at the lip corners; some of her tones quite bass in quality; her breath has a faint odor of humanity, of damp earth, of oak leaves, and she gives an impression of shivering or fluttering — whether she actually shivers I don't know, but somehow she gives that impression."

"But *the* characteristic of her face," Zaleski continued, his eyes still closed, in the voice of one entranced, "is that the top of her forehead, the bottom of her forehead, the lips, and the chin are all in one straight line when seen in profile — with only the nose projecting beyond the dead verticality of the face. And she has a mania which she preaches. Am I not right?"

"Yes," I answered, "her face is certainly as you say; and I suppose that her antipathy to all her countrymen, save Carlists, might be called a mania."

"So that," Zaleski said, "while we two are comfortably chatting here, the life of some outcast in the East End of London is steadily approaching death's door. It seems that we should make a move, Shiel."

Zaleski spread a map of London before me; a ring in red ink marked a small central area.

"Make a move?" I asked.

"Yes, for you must understand that, unless we successfully intervene, an assassination will take place tomorrow at about two hours after midnight on a certain Dene Street, near a certain charity Shelter there," — he pointed to the spot — "as the dates, hours, and places of the murders of the six London outcasts tell us. For the murderer's motive in assassinating those Londoners of both sexes and of the lowest class is not obscure, but stares us in the face: that motive is simply to throw dust in the eyes, and conceal the motive for the assassination of the seven Spaniards; for all the murders are either of London prostitutes and beggars, or of Spaniards, with the Spaniards being all officials, politicians, people of influence, serving the new King. The motive for killing them would have been evident, if their killings were not complicated, obscured, by the murders of London wastrels. And the order in which the murders have occurred cries out for our attention: first a Spaniard, *then* a London prostitute, beggar, or thief, like a sound and its echo, the Spaniards being 1, 3, 5, 7, 9, 11, 13, while the Londoners were 2, 4, 6, 8, 10, 12. Now, if it is assumed, as it has been, that the murders were all committed by one person, how inscrutable the motive of that person becomes! But you and I now perceive that the murders were done by two persons — by a son and by a mother, the mother's to make the motive of the son's inscrutable. Hence our need for making a move at once, for as I have noted and pointed out, all the murders of Londoners have occurred in the early-morning hours near a charity Shelter on Dene Street, of which Shelter the woman-assassin is, I feel sure, an official; she poses, no doubt, as a philanthropist, and is thus above suspicion."

Now Zaleski called aloud: "Ham, come!"

It was with a face of care that the Negro appeared; he had probably been listening to our talk, for he addressed his master, saying, "Do not go to her!"

"But suppose I thought that I must, Ham," — from the Prince.

And Ham: "Oh, good God, do not! I have a feeling — I have seen her face in a dream. Go and you never come back! Hear me this once — do not go!"

"It is true there is danger," Zaleski said smiling. It was clear that he was pleased by his servant's loyal concern. "But it is not danger to us, Ham."

The Prince moved to his ivory *escritoire* where he penned a few words on a sheet of paper and handed it to his anxious Ham, with the order to take my trap and drive with the message in all haste to the nearest telegraph office.

"That message," he said, resuming his place amid the cushions, "is the last word on the murders, and will, no doubt, insure their end. And now, Shiel, let us sit together and talk of more cosmic matters."

"But this murder that is to occur!" I protested.

"Quite so," said Zaleski calmly. "If our good Inspector Chamberlain is swift, it will be avoided. I have suggested a decoy to him — to surround Dene Street until dawn — and a search warrant for 7 Lens Crescent. Be at ease, Shiel — *la justice dérangera ton enfer.* This little affair is over. Let us now go on to matters of real concern, I beg. I see you, alas, far too seldom."

The suicide of Lady Poynting by a knife thrust to the heart when she was cornered in a mews off Dene Street, and the execution of her son, the Marquess of Markstow, with a silken rope, as befitted his rank, after Inspector Chamberlain had secured ample evidences of guilt in their rooms, including even a list of future victims, were "Society Sensations" that kept chatter long busy.

The Times announcing that a grateful King of Spain had bestowed the Golden Fleece on Zaleski, I wrote to congratulate him. He replied: "I sent it back, suggesting your name. Mundane affairs are not for me. Come soon, with or without a problem. How do you explain Wallace's *On Miracles* or that Ham is mastering the Art of the Omelette?"

But, alas, I was destined never to see my friend again. . . .

Cummings King Monk

He Meddles with Women

Apple tarts! Apple tarts!—HEINE

I once had occasion to hire a first floor in Bloomsbury, in one of those houses where the first floor is respectable, and the others but shabby genteel. It was there that I first saw Cummings King Monk, who occupied the top floor.

Without knowing his name, I would occasionally meet him on the stairs; but his name came out one day when I asked a servant who was carrying up a tray of letters if all those were for one person, and her answer was: "They are for Mr. Monk: every post brings him sixty or seventy."

I thought to myself: "Either this man is a begging letter-writer on a big scale, or a personage of great importance in the world," for I could see that the envelopes bore the crests of courts and clubs, and though some were but illiterately scribbled, on one I noticed the well-known autograph of an English prince.

The only other fact which I then knew about Monk was the fury with which he flew up and down stairs, three at a time. But soon afterwards it happened that I had invited two ladies to a "first night," could not obtain tickets, and was at a loss, when Monk one afternoon stopped me, saying that he had desired my acquaintance, had a box for the "first night," and — was I disposed to take it? I was!

Some weeks later he sent me down an invitation to dinner, and when I replied that it was impossible that evening, it was then that I first came into contact with this man's control over his fellow-creatures; for he sent me down a second note, informing me that De R—— had promised to make a third in our party, and concluded with the words: "Do not try to resist that inducement, since you will fail."

It was quite true: and I remember being struck by his knowledge of my passion for a particular art, for this particular artist, and the self-sure manner in which he had adapted the special bait to my special nature.

Monk strongly resembled the late Prince Consort — medium height, a figure lithe, slight, a browned countenance crowned by a brow livid-white and high, his hair curling forward in two curls about his ears in a quaint way; in one of the ears being a gold button, worn, I believe, for a weakness of the eyes. His manners were of an extreme feverishness, his speech keen, frequently even furious and voluminous.

I cannot refrain from mentioning an incident of that Café Royal dinner of ours.

De R—— wished to hear a certain "star," and Monk proposed that we should all go; we none of us, however, remembered which was the music-hall, the waiter was absent, no newspaper visible; but suddenly Monk said: "There is an old Major with a paper; we'll get that."

"But — he is reading it!" I said.

"He is reading one column, yes — has already read it thrice —" and he rose at once and stepped towards the Major, passing behind him, his eyes meanwhile peering into the paper. He then said: "May I ask, sir, if your paper contains a graphic account of the grand charge of which we are all talking?"

"Why, yes," the Major answered; "are you interested?"

"Acutely. It is a former servant of mine who has done the deed."

"What, Mackay? Is that so? Is it not a thrilling piece of work? If you were to read this description in *The Evening* ——"

"But I could hardly deprive you ——"

"Do not mention it," and as Monk was halfway back to our table, the Major called after him: "The Ensign Eversleigh who led the charge is — *my son!*"

All Monk said to us in explanation of his rape of the paper was that he had known that the Major was perusing something which touched his self-love. "He is quite happy now," he added, "in picturing to himself my rapture as I read."

Well, within a year I had gathered a good many facts concerning Monk — such as that he was of noble rank, had some Hebrew blood, and was among the six or seven wealthiest men. Fortune, he told me, had made of him a target, and, from his youth, had gunned him with gold, the estate of three millions left him in tail by his father forming a trifling item in the river of his revenues, the bulk being derived from a great-uncle of his mother, a Nürnberg Jew, who had invested his fortune for accumulation, designating as his heir a child to be born who should fulfil all the conditions fulfilled by Monk.

He was frequently to be met in the queerest dens, had a liking for Cockneyland, and in his pockets keys to five or six lodgings, into which he might dive and disappear.

As to the tone of his mind, I can describe it best by saying that Monk was a conjuror from his cradle, his conjuror's tools being now philosophic concepts, and now human beings.

This has been said of other men, of Richelieu, Bismarck; but

Richelieu, Bismarck, were conjurors by a figure of speech, not like the mummer I knew as Monk, who was anon a conjuror playing exactly with the self-consciousness, in the manner, and with the airs, of a paid conjuror, and in general with some recklessness of the cost or consequences of his play.

I will adduce an instance, it being understood that where I was not present, I had the facts from Monk himself.

Once when I dropped in upon him in a garret in a "court," he then bending over a pigmy grate reading Greek, "Bully of you to come," he broke out at once: "What do you think, now, of this man Orpheus? A musician who could play so sweet as to make trees jig!"

"Wasn't Orpheus rather a sun-myth?" I asked, sitting on the one chair, Monk being on the rug.

"Or he might quite well have been a man with headaches," he said, "who, if he didn't make trees jig, did do other similar things. Rather fascinating! And why? Because men guess that there are powers latent within their own brows boundlessly greater than they have ever been trained to show, and that here or there a man may have breathed by whom they were actually shown."

"We must have degenerated," I said. "Instead of Orpheus and his womenfolk swarming after his music, we have Kubelik and bouquets ——"

Monk smiled with, "You jest as to 'degenerated,' and you talk of women swarming! Why ——"

He stopped.

"Well?" I said.

"Stop — let me see. Could I? Would you like to see, my

friend, a swarm, all women, raging through London after one solitary male?''

He uttered it with a sudden flush! and I believe in that minute had schemed each detail of some whim which now filled him.

He clapped on his cleft felt hat, caught my arm, saying, ''Let's have some lunch. See if I don't show you something soon. . . .''

That evening a mysterious circumstance which created a sensation occurred at a ball of Lady Tw——, in Park Lane, I myself being as puzzled as anybody when I heard of it, although it certainly occurred to me that this might be but the first act in Monk's new comedy.

At this ball the Princess W—— of B——, in the oddest manner, lost her wedding-ring — a ring having an enormous fancy-value, owing to the fact that it had long been the badge of marriage in that family. On its surface was a scratch, cross-shaped.

The Princess W—— happened at the instant to be in conversation with the French Ambassador, two Countesses, Cummings King Monk, and a Reichs-Fürst. Early in the morning it was, they standing on a balcony hanging over a back garden that had some lanterns, only one electric jet in the leafy ceiling relieving the shadow; and the conversation had turned on the wedding-ring.

''Prince Henry,'' the Princess said, ''regards it with a sort of awe, like some genie ring.''

''By its magic he holds the Princess W——,'' observed the Ambassador.

"But one wonders whether its binding virtue lasts after so many bindings," said a Countess; "like those electric belts which run down ——"

"I fancy it holds my husband indifferently well," muttered the Princess with a shrug.

"A ring, the symbol of eternity, must be unaffected by time," observed Monk.

"Or improved by it," added the Ambassador, "like wine: for both bind friendship, and open a lady's tenderness."

"I must see the famous ring some day," said Monk.

"You would like ——?" asked the Princess. "Then, why not now?"

"Your glove ——"

"Doesn't matter. Though there is really nothing to *see*. . . ."

Talking still, she drew off her glove; and, talking still, half-averted, held out the little hand sideways, her fingertips resting on Monk's left hand, three of the fingers being now encrusted with a crowd of rings.

Monk bent over the hand, and touching a spot of the Princess's third finger with his own right forefinger, muttered: "This middle one must be it by the Ungar *mode*," but immediately added, "No, this is not it. *Which* is it?"

The Princess, turning, bent to show him. "This one," she said; and then immediately, "why, no; where is it?"

She bent lower, and now went pale.

Where was it? It had vanished. All flurried, she hurried into a room where there was light, the others following. She drew off the other glove, doubting her left hand and her right; then looked blankly about.

"It is not here."

"This is most strange!"

"It is incredible."

"But it is impossible!"

"How could you lose it?"

"It is not here."

"Are you sure?"

"It was just here."

"Where?"

"Where this ring now is."

"How remarkable!"

"But I don't remember this ring! Is it mine?"

"It must be."

"I suppose so. I was dressed so hurriedly ——"

"Have you had off the wedding-ring today?"

"Yes — once."

"Then, perhaps ——"

"No, I am sure that I put it on again."

"Ah, in that case—— But may you not have put on the other ring, thinking it somehow the wedding-ring?"

"I can't think that."

"Then, it is an amazing thing!"

The hostess came up. The alarm spread. The mystery was of such a kind that no mind could begin to divine it.

Monk found an opportunity to breathe at the Princess's ear:

"I hope you are not going to distress yourself. I even assure you that it must be found. Then your pleasure will more than repay you. . . ." But she was not to be comforted.

The next day the ring was the theme of the papers, which announced a reward of five-thousand pounds for its recovery.

It may be said at once that the loss of this ring was due to

Monk; and by nine-thirty that morning he was engaged in the second act of his drama, being then in an office in Hatton Garden, before him a portly Jew, to whom he was saying: "Now, look you, I am interested in this affair, Bernstein — have guaranteed the Princess that the ring shall be found, and so on. But, you see, it has nothing to identify it, except two scratches; and now that this reward is out, what is to prevent all England from buying wedding-rings, scratching crosses on them, and presenting them as the real ring. Think of the bother of it! We can't have that, you know."

"Oh, I follow you, Mr. Monk," lisped Bernstein, rubbing his plump palms, "and I take it that you want me to ——"

"Yes, to get out a circular quick — you are in such close touch with the trade — let no wedding-ring be sold, in London, anyway, for two days. You will undertake a three-and-half percent reimbursement on profits for every ring refused to be sold by the retailer, and I reimburse you at four — Oh, look at the oil of gladness on his face now! But, hullo! I don't see that nephew of yours anywhere."

"You don't want to insult a man, Mr. Monk, I'm sure," was Bernstein's answer to this.

"Insult? What, because he got those six months, you mean? But where's the good of playing the Pharisee before a man like me? I bet if Sam were to come to you with one of his fetching schemes in an hour's time, you'd finance him! And who could blame you?"

"Well, he knows his way about, and that's the truth, does Sam," said Bernstein, softening. "But still — don't mention the gaol-bird's name to me, sir, I beg!"

"So where's he now?"

"Oh, shamming sick at one of the hospitals, I believe."

"Which one?"

"St. Thomas's."

"I think I shall look up the poor devil, Bernstein, and give him a job. Be prompt, now, about stopping sale of rings," and he rushed out to his cab, calling out, "St. Thomas's Hospital!" — Sam Bernstein being the next pawn in this game. And presently Monk was sitting by a bedside in the "Caroline" ward, saying to Sam, "Well, Sam Bernstein, shamming sick again?"

"Anything for a quiet life, Mr. Monk," answered Sam on his elbow, adding: "To what may I owe the favor of this visit, sir?"

His eyes examined Monk — a wizened wight, true Cockney, true Jew, true criminal, impishly shrewd of face, with fleshly lips, and matted black locks hanging about his pallid countenance; while a rattle in his chest showed that his illness was not wholly a sham.

"The favor of my visit?" said Monk. "Why not drop that whine? Your uncle was just telling me that you are down in the world ——"

"Moy loif, been to my uncle so early in the morning, Mr. Monk?"

"And have some move on, of course — you suspicious wretch. You might guess why I went —— Or haven't you heard of the robbery?"

Sam's interest instantly quickened. He sat up.

"Robbery?"

"Well, the Princess W—— lost her wedding-ring last night, and there's a reward of five thousand ——"

"Moy loif!"

"I happen to be interested, so hurried to your uncle Bernstein to get him to stop sale of wedding-rings for a day or two."

"Stop sale — what's the deal, Mr. Monk?"

"Why, where are your wits?" asked Monk. "The lost ring has only two scratches to identify it; anybody could counterfeit it — provided he could get a ring to buy."

Sam lay back, pondering this, not a wrinkle on his forehead, but his eyes as alive as lightning.

And the tempter went on: "Another thing — the Princess *says* she lost the ring last night, because she missed it last night; but, of course, it may have been lost five years ago. A married woman isn't always looking at her ring — knows it is there all right — doesn't trouble. So that, suppose Mrs. Brown or Mrs. Jones has a wedding-ring with some scratch on it, the first thing she will think is that hers may be the very Princess's ring, stolen long ago, and bought by Jones for her. Then, of course, she presents her ring as the lost one."

Sam was all interest now; he muttered half to himself, "No fear about women parting with their wedding-rings for any money — bad luck! But *the husbands* might be got at, though. Only I don't quite see where a deal would come in ——"

The tempter smiled, saying, "True, the husbands; *they'd* part with their wives' wedding-rings for five-thousand pounds lightly enough. And that's why I'm afraid of someone or other perpetrating a fraud on those same husbands this day."

"Fraud?" muttered Sam with irritation; "strike me silly! I don't see through the game."

"Why, it stares you in the face," said Monk. "Well, you wouldn't do such a thing yourself — I'll tell you. First of all, where do you suppose the Princess's ring is at this moment?"

Sam's lips twitched. "Where, sir?"

"On her finger, I imagine — though I have a reason of my own for not giving her the hint for some days."

"Finger?"

"Who could get it off, without her knowing — except her husband? and he's in France. I'd almost swear that someone had a motive for changing her wedding-ring into another kind of ring while it was on her finger."

"But — how?" Sam's stare was like a cat's over a mouse-hole.

"Why, where *are* your wits today?" asked Monk. "What's simpler than to clap upon a wedding-ring a row of stones like this" — he exhibited from his purse a curve of turquoises, the big one in the middle containing a pigmy magnet and a piston of soft iron to create a vacuum — "any goldsmith's 'prentice could make you one in an hour. You take a curve of seven gems glued together, gems tapering in size toward each end of the curve; and you drill a tunnel in the big middle gem, a tunnel from the inside face of the gem toward the outside face, a tunnel nearly as long as the gem's depth, a quarter of an inch long, say, and a sixteenth in diameter; then at the tunnel's closed end you fire a little bar-magnet the sixteenth of an inch long, and into the tunnel you insert a little rod of soft iron, a true fit with the tunnel, kept in position by friction, the eighth of an inch long. So, if you now press the curve of gems against a wedding-ring (which has no gems), the ring will press against the projecting end of the rod, pushing the rod further into the tunnel to the influence of the magnet, which, in drawing the rod, will create a vacuum between rod-end and ring; and air-pressure on the outer face of the gems — fifteen pounds per square inch — about an ounce in this case — will fix the curve of gems to the ring. And *now* do you see how the husbands of half England could be swindled in this affair? But it doesn't concern you, Sam Bernstein. What I came to tell you is that, if you care to do some copying for me, I can give you a job."

A change had passed over Sam's face; for where the deal came in he could see, and, for an instant could not conceal an aspect of keenness as of the cat wriggling to spring; but then said wearily, "I am feeling so bad, Mr. Monk, of late. Copying, I don't think, wouldn't hardly suit me, though sorry I am ——"

"Then — I'm off," Monk said, rising. "You are very independent, my friend. I suppose it's because you know that Uncle Bernstein will receive you with open arms, the first good thing you have to put before him — what?" and he was gone.

He was probably no sooner out than Bernstein bounded from bed; and the same hour had claimed a Briton's liberty, and was out, bound for his Uncle Bernstein's.

All that day he was blissfully busy, like a liberated being revelling in its own element once more; his consumption vanished; he had talks with his uncle, in which they bent together, with magnifiers imbedded in their eye-sockets, over little curves of turquoises; he visited his acquaintances, and they sat gravely together in cabinet-councils; he hired in haste three offices — in Westminster, in Bishopsgate, and in Whitechapel — and in each he had carpenters hammering; he left at newspaper offices this advertisement: "Whoever is the happy possessor of a wedding-ring with a scratch should bring it to one of the three following addresses for identification. Five-thousand pounds reward."

Before nightfall London began to feel the influence of his

energies — and to respond to it. By the next morning there was trouble.

I, personally, came into contact with the results of Mr. Sam Bernstein's activities several times that day — without any suspicion of their significance. First, in passing out in the morning, I was asked by my housekeeper if I had happened to see anything of — a ring. "It is nonsense asking, I know," she added.

"No," I said, "what kind of ring?"

"My wedding-ring! It hasn't been off my finger this five-and twenty years" — and, in truth, I could see the pale place on her finger where the ring had pressed it.

"It's the queerest thing!" she cried out. "I could almost take my oath that it was on my finger last night; yet this morning when I woke it was gone!"

And again, about 3 P.M., at Oxford Circus, I witnessed the meeting of two girls, from one of whom, in the act of shaking hands, burst the words, "Where's your wedding-ring?"

"My dear, it's lost! But how quick you notice!"

"Haven't I cause?" said the first. "Both Maude Wilson and my Kit lost theirs during the night; and now yours, too!"

The very expression of mystification kept their lips agape. I, for my part, somehow had a thought of Monk, and the women-crowds of Orpheus; but it was but momentary, since it was not possible to conceive how *he* could have a hand in this.

And again at Clapham that night, while writing a postcard in a stationer's shop, I noticed that the woman of the establishment was looking about, under the counter, everywhere, with a face of worry. So I asked if she had lost anything.

"My wedding-ring!" leapt from her lips.

She had missed it from her finger that morning about nine.

This miracle so pricked my wonderment that I went hunting for Monk that night at several of his haunts, but failed to find him. It was not till the next morning that I first saw Mr. Sam Bernstein's advertisement: "Whoever is the happy possessor of a wedding-ring should bring it to one of the following addresses. . . ." but this brought no light to my mind, since at the time I was ignorant even of the existence of Sam.

Anyhow, those "three addresses" were during three days besieged by a crowd, all males, from morning to night; for the reward was five-thousand pounds, and at the advertisement of Bernstein, who was assumed to be some authorized agent of the Princess, fevered became the agitation, each of not less than twenty thousand London men conceiving the hope that Chance might pick *him* out as the possessor of the lost ring. Some, acting in bad faith, rushed to jeweller after jeweller, but failed to obtain a wedding-ring to scratch, since Monk had stopped their sale; others, acting in good faith, imagined a scratch on their wife's ring, and believed it not impossible that it might prove to be the Princess's, lost perhaps long previously; and all, in the end, by one means or another — during her sleep, by some ruse or scheme — got hold of their helpmeet's pledge of wedlock, to wend hopefully with it to those addresses of Bernstein's advertisement; but every one went away with a face fretted with perplexity and dismay.

Bernstein's three offices had all been partitioned into compartments, each to hold one man only in its dingy cell, Sam or one of his gang standing behind the rude counter, leaning over a ledger on whose leaves lay strewn jewels and rings — none of them wedding-rings; nor did Sam look up from his writing when

Brown entered from the queue outside; he said only, "Fill up this form," and "Name, please."

Brown gave his name, meantime depositing his ring among the others on the ledger, which completely covered the strip of counter.

"Address, please."

It was given, the shopman wrote it in the ledger, and now straightened himself up to ask: "Where's the ring?"

"There," said Brown, with a hovering finger.

"*Where?*"

"Why, didn't I put it there?"

"I don't see it."

Brown's fingers began to fumble in his pockets.

"Hurry up, please," says the shopman, who, while Brown had been preoccupied between writing and answering, had by the motion of a fingertip pushed a concave of jewels to stick to the convex of Brown's ring.

And after one minute's contention Brown was both believing the incredible, and disbelieving all things: he had lost the ring on his way — his eyes were a lie — the universe was lunatic. He went away with a bowed brow of worry, moody, mute, still fumbling in his waistcoat, boring his way through the waiting multitude straining for admittance. It was Sam Bernstein's "deal." By the end of the second day he owned a sum of thirty-thousand pounds sterling in wedding-rings.

He took the precaution, however, in view of the Law, to attach for the present to every ring a ticket, bearing the name and address of its owner.

But on the third day there was a hitch, when one of his customers — a man with a Yankee beard and a sombrero —

happened to step into the very cell where Sam himself bent over the ledger.

"Name, please," said Sam to him.

"John P. Wood."

"Address."

"No. 9, Keppel Street."

Sam wrote it, and straightened himself.

"Where's the ring?"

"*There!*" answered the man, and pointed definitely.

At once Bernstein lost nerve, turning ashen.

"But that's not a wedding-ring, my good man, can't you see?" he whined with reproach. "It belongs ——"

"To *me,* and it is a wedding-ring, Sam, with some stones stuck on it."

Upon which the man made a snatch at Sam's beard, pulling it off, at the same time pulling off his own. And Sam staggered; his twitching lips wished to spit out, *"Mr. Monk!"* but could utter nothing.

"So this is the use you make of my chance chat with you, you jackal!" said Monk. "Quick, Sam — quick, lad — three years for this, unless you hand over to me each and all of those rings within the half-hour! The books first!"

Sam had collapsed; and presently was accompanying Monk in a cab to his other offices, which Monk left bearing several cash-boxes crammed with ticketed rings.

A thundering banging made by somebody in distracted haste sounded at my door that night about nine. When I looked out in wonder, Monk shouted irritably from below: "Come quick! — never mind about hats!"

I bounded down, and was away with him, he quite breathless,

red with ecstasy, and, as we dived into a cab, cries he to the driver: ''Five pounds to get us to the Mansion House within seven minutes!''

In the cab he showed me an advertisement, inserted by himself in the papers that day: ''Let lady who has lost wedding-ring meet advertiser before Mansion House at nine sharp this evening. She will recover, free of cost. Husband, show this to your wife.''

But we were late, and all the time he held watch on palm, as up Holborn we dashed at a gallop; and we had hardly got to St. Martin's, when we saw that something had thrown the traffic into one mass of confusion, no passage anywhere, cabmen fiercely vociferating, policemen fretfully busy.

''Come — can't wait!'' muttered Monk to me, jumping out, and away he dashed, forgetting to pay, dashed back again in a passion of haste, and we were off anew on foot, up Cheapside, dodging amid the wheels of the long block of vehicles in the middle of the street — for the pavements were thronged — dodging through billows. And all the while I knew not at all what the to-do was about! but suddenly saw — for all that space between the Mansion House, the Stock Exchange and the Bank was one sea of people; and away down each street leading from the space one could perceive vistas of people teeming; and they were nearly all women, some twenty thousand, come to meet Cummings Monk.

By the largeness of the thing, all the oddity of it, my consciousness was somehow utterly bewildered. The air was full of tongues and rumors — but sounding in a tone quite *outré,* high, unusual with crowds. I remember that, in the midst of my bewilderment of mind, a singular giddiness, a quite wild kind of gaiety, somehow struck me, for something electric was about, some bacchic influence, emanating from the crowd. I saw it in the face of Monk, from whom I had got somewhat separated; I saw it on the faces of the scores of constables. Monk was then in the center of a number of inspectors and constables, some of whom evidently knew him, explaining something to them, and I saw him hand round something — money possibly — whereupon the officers separated, and went disseminating some message among the ladies. At the same time Monk bored his way to a four-wheeler near the Exchange, and standing erect on the seat, began some harangue, which my ear could not exactly catch, though I understood that he was assuring them that their rings were in his hands, and that, given the chance, he would deliver them up that very day.

Then, as he leapt down and moved, there were shooting fingers at him, shouts of ''That's he! that's he!'' and I heard one woman say earnestly to another: ''Whatever you do, don't let him out of your sight this night!''

Monk now started out on a deliberate walk down Cheapside, where the crowd was thinner, and where the police had by now organized a pathway between the vehicles down the middle of the street; whereupon some few of the ladies came after Monk, and soon there ensued a definite movement, a large tendency flowing after him, then a march, a rolling Rhone, the mass of an army's tramp. By the time we were at Bennet's Clock, a decided tide of life was on the move, Cummings Monk the moon that moved it. I forced my way towards him.

Suddenly, coming from Lime Street, a company of lads who had some tin fifes and a drum, crossed Monk's path; and at once he pounced upon the drummer, whispered doubtless some one of his wizard words, quickly had the drum hanging round his own throat, and began to batter at it.

"Follow the music!" — backward he flung this howl; and soon in the mass of the crowd there arose a rumor of *"Follow the music!"* while on by St. Martin's, down Holborn, the host flowed after the rattle of his ran-tan, four work-girls going ahead of him whirling in dance, hurling jests at the multitude, on each side of Monk a policeman, one of them — a plump lump — stepping in a rhythmic way with a swinging head, solemn! — as ridiculous a thing, I think, as I ever saw; and anon, far-repeated in the rear would arise the cry and rumor of *"Follow the music!"*

Monk spoke to me without ceasing in a species of shout. Here and now he was happy, in contact with humanity, warm, nourished, gushing with comradeship, nor have I ever known him so blushing with gaiety, or glib with wit, and ever his mass of femaledom, flanked by policemen, teemed far-reaching after him, drawn by his nimble drumstick's rumbling — on down Oxford Street, to Southampton Row, and thence up into Russell Square. Here Monk leapt up the doorsteps of his house near a corner, so hard-pressed from behind, that he had hardly time to fumble in his key, slip within, and slam the door. Outside there were cries, a crush, one woman fainted: and without delay the square was flooded and a-sound.

When he appeared on the balcony, wearing still his little split-hat and his drum stuck on his stomach, someone holding a lamp by him, he was recognized with a great, vague tumult and movement of the women like wind within the woods. He came to the rail, leaned his fists on it, and presently the sounding square stilled down a little round him.

"Ladies!" he shouted, "you now see where I live — my bachelor home! Let that for tonight satisfy you, since it is impossible with my own hands to distribute your rings among you in a moment. Thousands of you, ladies! Imagine the nature of my sensations at this moment! My heart cannot count you — you embarrass me — I am become the paragon of patriarchs and sultans. And henceforth my prayer shall be, 'Thy Lesbos come!' For don't you know that ancient lists of names, such as biblical lists, show that the earth in the bigness of her early vigor turned out more men than women? then as many women? and now more women? So we need but go on to behold this globe one blessed Lesbos; and may you and I then be here again. But what I have to tell you in all seriousness is that your rings are safe. I have here behind me an army of clerks directing envelopes, and every one of you may be certain of having back her own identical ring tomorrow first thing (Vast Applause), accompanied for all your trouble and travel by a little half-sovereign. I have only, then, to thank each of you most heartily for coming to meet me, to ask you to disperse like good girls, and to wish you a sincere — Good night." He stepped backward, bowing, amid a shouting of bravos, and shower of flowers rent from many a breast.

It may be added that the Princess W—— got that same day an anonymous letter, telling her that a little tug would get off the row of stones from her wedding-ring.

He Defines "Greatness of Mind"

Come, now, and let us reason together.—ISAIAH

This indeed appears to me to be a beautiful thing, if someone is able to instruct men, like Gorgias the Leontine, and Hippias the Elian: for each of these, in the cities which he visits, has the power of persuading the young men, who give him money, and thanks besides, for his instruction.

—SOCRATES

On a night in December when Monk dined with me, he wore a shade over his eyes, and was quiet and subdued — a mood in which I liked him best, since then instruction was sure to come for me from his strong forehead. But in dining I happened to make some remark as to Cardinal Newman, to which my friend answered: "Well, but Newman was a savage": whereupon I could not but exclaim against the use of such a word to designate such a personage. Monk, however, it turned out, had not used the word as some loose semi-expression of a moment's sentiment, but strictly, as a term in a scientific proposition; and he replied to me: "Since you deny that Newman was a savage, it is for you to tell me what you say that a savage is."

As we had just then risen from dinner, I took a dictionary, and read out to him: "Savage — a human being uncivilized: one of a brutal, unfeeling disposition."

This caused Monk to laugh! and he said: "But are not dictionaries made by leisured gentlemen in a state of hibernation?

143

especially that one which you have in your hand, in which, if you look out 'high,' you will find 'not low,' and if you then with anxiety look out 'low,' you will find 'not high.' Is that inspired to define a savage as 'one of a brutal disposition' when tribes assuredly savage have been known for mildness? the Caribs, for instance? 'the mild-eyed, melancholy Lotus-eaters'?''

"No," I answered; "but there remains the other definition: 'a human being uncivilized.'"

"Notice the poetical position of 'uncivilized'!" he laughed. . . . "So, then, that is your definition? . . . 'a savage is an uncivilized human adult'? Very good. But as to the ex-Sultan of Turkey, now: was he a civilized person, or an uncivilized?"

"Uncivilized," I answered after some thought.

"A savage, then?"

"Well, yes."

"And as to a navvy of Whitechapel who can't read: a civilized person or an uncivilized?"

"Uncivilized."

"A savage, then?"

"I suppose that I must say so."

"But as to Plato of Athens," he said, "civilized or uncivilized?"

"Civilized, certainly," I answered.

"Not a savage?"

"No."

"Was Cato the Younger?"

"No."

"Is Mr. Bernard Shaw?"

"No."

"Was Julius Caesar?"

"No."

"Was Dante?"

"No."

"Was Milton?"

"No."

"But," he said, "the difference betwixt a savage and one not a savage must be considerable: what, then, is it which makes so much difference betwixt Plato and the Sultan that Plato was not a savage, but the Sultan is one?"

"This," I answered: "that Plato represented the utmost culture of his age — mental, moral, sociable, physical; but the Sultan has not attained the utmost culture of his age, at any rate, moral: for he encourages massacres, and is dubbed Abdul the Damned."

"So, then," said Monk, "a person who has not attained the utmost culture of his age — mental, moral, sociable, physical — is an uncivilized person, or savage?"

"Yes," I answered, "more or less."

"Well," he said, "we have come to something now! for first you defined 'savage' as 'an uncivilized' person, and now you define 'uncivilized' person: he is a person who has not attained the utmost culture of his age in those four respects. Now, Plato did, perhaps: so I understand now why you say that Plato was not a savage, but the Sultan is one. But as to Lord Rosebery: is he one?"

"No," I answered.

"Yet," said Monk, "Lord R—— has not attained the physical culture of Maude Allan, the utmost of his age: is not his lordship, therefore, a savage?"

"No," I said: "it appears that I must leave out the physical: civilization, I now say, is in respect only of mental, moral, and sociable culture."

"Well!" said Monk: "but it is not to be supposed that Lord Rosebery has attained the moral culture of a Sister Agnes Jones or a Newman, the utmost of his age, nor quite the sociable culture of an *exquis* like Oscar Wilde, the utmost of his age; and Carlyle, we know, could be something of a boor. Are not his lordship, then, and Carlyle, savages?"

"No, no," I answered: "I see that I must leave out the moral and the sociable, as the physical; and the mental remains: so I say that 'a savage is a person who has not attained the utmost mental culture of his age.'"

"But in that case," said Monk, "the Sultan may not be a savage, though he encourages massacres."

"Well, but he is one," I insisted, "everybody calls him so: for, obviously, one must have *some* moral culture, or one is a savage."

"But how much moral culture?" asked Monk: "as much as Lord Rosebery? or less? or more?"

"About as much as Lord Rosebery," I answered: "that is to say, the average moral culture of his age."

"Very good," said Monk, "I mark that much. But as to Carlyle, now: if, instead of being merely rather Presbyterian, he had eaten like Johnson, nor ever washed himself, would he not have been savage?"

"Yes," I answered, "for one, obviously, must have *some* sociable and physical culture, in order not to be savage."

"But how much sociable and physical culture? As much as Carlyle? or less? or more?"

"About as much as Carlyle: that is to say, the average sociable and physical culture of his age."

"Quite so," he said: "but as you have now made some changes, you had better define 'savage' afresh, so that we may understand where we are."

"Well," I said, "we appear to have reached to this: that 'a savage is a person who has not attained the utmost mental, and the average moral, sociable, and physical culture of his age.'"

"But," said Monk, "just think: is Rosebery's 'mental culture' — whatever that means — equal to Spencer's, the utmost of his age? You will not say so. Yet his lordship is not, because of that, a savage?"

"No," I said, "for Spencer's culture, if higher, is not immensely the higher: and a somewhat lower culture does not justify so lush an adjective as 'savage.'"

"Then," said Monk, "you should pack that into your definition: for we wish to be exact."

"A savage, then," I said, "is a person who is *far* from having attained the *utmost* mental, and the *average* moral, sociable, and physical culture of his age."

"Good," said Monk: "I now love our definition better, and by still bungling about it we may get it on its legs in the end. But I am still somewhat against it. What, for example, does *culture* mean? I am never quite certain and clear: it is such a pliant kind of word, except when applied to plants and land. So, for my sake, could you not find some other word than 'culture'?"

"What other word?" I said: "'refinement'? 'attainment'? I don't know."

"But," said Monk, "what is the *note* of culture? in what

respect does a cultured rose specifically differ from an un-cultured? a cultured muscle, a cultured skull, from an un-cultured?''

"The cultured is always the larger," I answered.

"Or at all events," he said, "can we not always say that it is somehow 'the more developed'?''

"We can," I answered.

"So let us say 'development' instead of 'culture,'" said he.

"All right," I answered.

"Or, instead of 'development' shall we not say 'evolution,' Shiel? since the two mean one thing?''

"Since that pleases you," I said, "we shall say 'evolution.'''

"So what now is a savage?" he demanded.

"A savage," I answered, "is 'a person who is *far* from having attained the *utmost* mental, and the *average* moral, sociable, and physical *evolution* of his age.'''

"But of *his* age!" exclaimed Monk, "surely that is a slip of your tongue. Was there not, then, an age when all mankind were naked savages?''

"Why, yes," I answered.

"And was not any one of those savages, though he had attained the utmost evolution of *his* age, still a savage in *your* view?''

"Yes, of course," I answered; "I see that I must change the definition yet again, and give it as: 'a savage is a person who is far from having attained the utmost mental, and the average moral, sociable, and physical evolution of the most evolved age, that is, of this age.'''

"Well," said Monk: "But tell me: is it not odd that in order not to be savage a man must approach to the 'utmost' mental evolution of this age, but need only approach to the 'average' moral, sociable, and physical evolution? Yet moral evolution, for example, is a most important matter, is it not? How, then, is this?''

''I don't know how it is,'' I answered, ''but it does seem to be so: for we have already seen that Lord Rosebery is not a savage, even though his moral evolution may be far from the utmost, inasmuch as his mental evolution is not far.''

''Yes,'' said Monk, ''I don't deny that it is so; I only say that it seems strange, and I inquired the reason, though I can see that the reason is suggested in our definition itself by the words 'this age.' ''

''In what way?'' I asked.

''Tell me,'' he said: ''is not a savage a relative thing? A Bushman is not a savage to a Bushman, but he is one to a Basuto? and a Basuto is one to you?''

''Yes.''

''And a cart-horse is not a savage to a cart-horse, but he is one to an Ascot-horse, no doubt? and a donkey to a cart-horse, no doubt? As, then, animals ascend a definite step in development, those on the steps just below get the name of 'savage': so, given a condition of things in which no evolution was going on, a savage would not occur, for, that there may be worse, there must be better. But with respect to the moral, sociable, and physical among men, there has been no evolution during ages, meaning that ages since particular standards and averages were reached in these respects which remain much the same, and may so remain for ages more. St. John, for example, was hardly less holy than Newman, nor St. Catherine than Sister Dora; Alcibiades was probably quite as die-away a cock as Oscar

Wilde; and an Olympiad champion as fit as Jackson — some think fitter. In holiness, then, in sociableness, and in physical fitness, a particular average and a particular ideal were attained in antiquity which have remained practically fixed, so that no modern man even aspires to be holier, politer, or fitter than the holiest, politest, or fittest of those times. Since, then, in these respects, there has been little or no evolution, there has been little savagery; for the savagery of some is relative to the evolution of others. The mass of men have settled down at a not very variable average of moral, sociable, and physical evolution, and only when some rare fish tumbles well below this average do we dub him a savage, as you dubbed the Sultan. And not only is this average and this ideal fixed and oldish, it is practically universal on the earth. I assume that a Yogi, or a mahatma, is as holy as Newman; a mandarin can be quite as exquisite as Oscar Wilde; and a Japanese champion has matched Hackenschmidt. So, in these respects, there has been no breezy pioneering and large-minded Alp-climbing by any regiment of the army of man, leaving the less adventurous regiments in the rear in the morass of savagery; and the pioneers toward the ideal are so scanty, that in the eyes of the mass a kind of fantasticality even attaches to a mahatma, a Wilde, or a Hackenschmidt. But with respect to mental development, is not the case different? Are we not better than our fathers, Shiel, and the Chinese?''

''Yes,'' I said, ''that is very much so. But still, Monk, I am not quite enlightened as to why it is that a man is not a savage who is far from the highest, say, moral evolution, though he has the average: for evolution is evolution: and if a mahatma is a savage who is far from the mental evolution of Lord Rosebery, then, Lord R. should be a savage compared with a mahatma, because far from the moral evolution of a mahatma.''

"But," said Monk, "do you say that Lord R. is a savage compared with a race-horse, because he is far from being able to run so fast?"

"No: there is no comparison."

"But do you say that a cart-horse is a savage compared with a race-horse because he is far from being able to run so fast?"

"Yes."

"But do you say that a race-horse is a savage compared with a mine-horse, because he is far from being able to see so well in the dark?"

"Certainly not."

"And do you not refuse to say this because you understand that the evolution of a horse is specially in the direction of running? not specially in the direction of seeing in the dark?"

"Yes."

"But the evolution of a man is not specially in the direction of running? but of something else?"

"Yes."

"In the direction of what else is it?" he asked.

"In the directions," I replied, "of thinking, of being holy, of being polite, and of being fit."

"But," said Monk, "in the directions of being holy, of being polite, and of being fit, no modern man has evolved beyond Hebrews and Greeks, nor even beyond people grossly savage: I know, for instance, an old negress in the Indies who is as holy as Sister Dora; and as regards the growing lad, we know that he is sometimes no more holy, polite, or fit at fifteen than he was at nine. In these respects, I say, evolution nods; there has been no evolution for long. Yet man has been rapidly evolving. In what direction, then, specially, is the evolving of man?"

"In the direction of thinking," I answered.

"Just as the evolving of horses is in the direction of running, Shiel?"

"So it certainly seems to be," I observed.

"Man, then," said Monk, "is an animal formed to think always more wondrously as horses to run always more wondrously. He is, moreover, an animal formed to be holy, to be sociable, and to be fit, but not somehow specially formed for these things, but for thinking, as horses may very conveniently haul carts, and see in the dark, but are hardly somehow specially formed for these ruts, but for running. So Lord Rosebery is no savage for being far from having the holiness of a mahatma and the muscle of a Sandow, since holiness and muscle are not somehow in the special footpath of man's evolution, but thinking, and since the most evolved men are hardly the holiest, most sociable, or fittest, but the most thoughtful. In this respect, then, I think, your definition stands solid: that 'a savage is a person who is far from having attained the *utmost* mental, and the *average* moral, sociable, and physical evolution of this age.' However, in other respects the definition does not stand so satisfactory: it is negative, for instance, giving what a savage is not, not what he is. But it should not be difficult to you to pull it into a positive definition."

"Well," I said, "since 'a person who is far from having attained the highest mental evolution of our age' is a person of primitive mind, I now define a savage as 'a person of primitive mind, or one who is far from having attained the average moral, sociable, and physical evolution of the historic ages.'"

"But *primitive mind* is so vague," replied Monk.

"Let us say, then, an undeveloped, an unevolved mind," I said.

"But 'unevolved' is again negative," he objected.

"What, then, shall I say, Monk?"

"But what," he said, "is an *unevolved* person? What were you and I twenty years ere we evolved into what we are?"

"By Zeus, Monk, we were children," I answered.

"Shall we not, then, Shiel, define a savage as 'a person of childish mind as compared with the most evolved minds, or one who is far from having attained the average moral, sociable, and physical evolution of the historic ages'?"

"We will," I answered: "though 'childish' itself seems vague, if not so vague as my 'primitive.'"

"Yes, 'childish,' too, is vague," he answered; "but will not all its vagueness vanish the moment we recall to mind the known notes of a child's mind?"

"Let us, then, recall these notes to mind," I said.

"We will," he said; "and is not the chief of them a certain *skittishness,* levity, irrelevance? due to an unconsciousness of facts? a certain kicking-up of the heels, for one's own part, at the vague universe? seen in the filly, the kid, the kitten? in the grown cat also? the grown horse in spring? the gorilla? and in the black of the Congo who cocks a battered top-hat on his head, and, naked else, rakishly promenades, so arranged, to parade his charm?"

"Yes," I said, "there is that skittishness in children."

"But how as to credulity?" he next said. "Is not this another note of a child's mind?"

"Very much so," I answered.

"Will not a child catch at almost any statement made to it, and rest upon that as upon a prop, to prop its wee weak top? just as in learning to walk it catches hold of the first thing? Or as a fledgling flutters down upon the first shrub? But when it has evolved to the Harrow age, it is already much more sceptical? and will ask questions if any strange thing be told it?''

''That is quite true,'' I said.

''Do you say, then, that scepticism is the bloom of mental evolution, as pear-trees are sure to bear pear-blooms?''

''From this of the growing child it must be recognized to be very much so,'' I replied.

''But as to the other known notes of a child's mind,'' said Monk, ''is not *over-belief* one of them?''

''Over-belief?'' I said. ''Is not that credulity?''

''But a very special example of it,'' he answered. ''Credulity is a weak-minded leaning upon the statements of others, as upon a crutch, or prop; but over-belief is a weak-minded leaning upon the adumbrations and presentations of one's own brain. When in the West Indies seven months since, I met many instances of it among the infantiles there. For example, funerals there are on foot, and after a time the funeral-train naturally becomes a little flurried, the driver of the coffin-cart shakes his reins a little, and the pace quickens; well, at such a moment one mourner will remark to another, 'Ah, poor thing, ain't she (the corpse) eager to get home?' 'True, true,' will be the answer, 'she's hurrying home, she's hurrying home.' Or take this: One dark night a ship-of-war, cruising off the north coast of St. Lucia, flashed its searchlight ashore, striking terror into the natives, and the workers in a certain 'boiling-house' (where sugar is boiled) were bounding frantically about, very like a troop of ecstatic baboons, when a son of the 'overseer' flew to howl in at the door, '*Pa!* Ma tell you come home quick, let's all die together!' To this, however, the stout old overseer answered, 'Boy, go back home and tell your mother dere's plenty of time before morning. It's only the antichrist; for the Word of God say the sea has got to burn up first.' Now, this is not story, but history; and think of the whole cloud-town of belief, its streets and squares laid out, springing up at the apparition of a ship's flashlight; the very succession of events on Judgment Day, now come, established in the otherwise blank consciousness, like a photo flashed over it by the fancy, and weakly accepted by it as authentic. And is not this a chief note of a child's mind?''

''It is so,'' I assented.

''But how as to stubbornness?'' he said: ''is not this another one of them?''

''Stubbornness?'' I said.

''Yes, for do we not know of 'the strength of childhood's impressions?' and how a mind which does not much evolve with time, but continues childish, clings to its initial beliefs with a stubbornness of the crab's claw, equal to the indifference with which it received them? and so all round resembling the crab's claw? which troubles not about what it grips, but, having gripped something, hugs it grimly? You who have not visited negroes can't even conceive the really infinite scorn with which a Catholic negro regards a Methodist, and a Methodist a Catholic. It would be in vain for the Methodist to attempt to convince the Catholic of the simplest fact, or the Catholic the Methodist, for the acceptance of first impressions has been so perfect that anyone who, in any respect, has received a different impression seems merely weak-headed to him. This stubbornness, then, you will say, is a chief note of a child's mind.''

''This, too,'' I assented.

''So, then,'' said Monk, ''our definition is no longer vague?

but we can say with conviction that 'a savage is a person of comparatively skittish, credulous, over-believing, stubborn mind — in a word, of childish mind — or one who is far from having attained the average moral, sociable, and physical evolution of the historic ages'?''

"We can say this with conviction," I said.

"Then," he said, "let us test by the definition as it now stands the judgments which you have pronounced upon particular persons. The Sultan of Turkey, for instance: is he still a savage?''

"Yes," I said, "for is he not far below the average moral evolution of the historic ages, since he encourages massacres?''

"Well, let that be so," he said. "But as to Julius Caesar; is he still not a savage?''

"Caesar was a great mind," I said. "A great mind cannot be a savage mind.''

"I fully agree with you in that," answered Monk, "for a great mind is certainly a strong mind; and we have seen that a savage mind is a childish, that is, a weak mind, trying to think like the wee weak knees of children trying to toddle. But are you sure, my friend, that Julius Caesar was a great mind?''

"Are not you?" I said. "Is not Caesar recognized as the greatest mind of antiquity — a general, an architect, a statesman, and other things?''

"He may have been so," answered Monk, "but mark that it is not antiquity that is now calling him 'a great mind,' but *you;* and this, I confess, seems to me undignified of you. Is it not, then, a fact that 'au royaume des aveugles les borgnes sont rois'? I, for my part, understand that there is scarce at this moment an English schoolboy who is not a greater general, a greater architect, a greater statesman, a greater mind than Caesar. Does it seem to you that I should undertake a long and difficult thing, if I undertook to prove this to you?''

''By Zeus, Monk, it does seem so to me,'' I said.

''Yet I think not,'' said Monk. ''Let us, then, see. But to begin, let us get to an agreement as to what a great mind is. What *is* it?''

''One that is least like a savage's or child's mind,'' I said.

''Precisely so,'' he said; ''least like the child's, the savage's, the gibbon's, the bee's, the amoeba's mind. The mind, then, that is more *mindly,* so to say, than other minds, in which the quality of *mindliness* is more evolved? But now, what is the special trait of Mind, from the mind of plants to the mind of man?''

''Consciousness,'' I said.

''And consciousness is a perception of facts?'' he asked.

''Yes,'' I said.

''And since greatness of mind is a great evolution of the quality of mindliness, and the trait of mindliness in consciousness, and consciousness is a perception of facts, does greatness of mind, then, consist in a great faculty of perceiving facts?''

''It does,'' I agreed.

''And in nothing else?''

''No, there is nothing else,'' I said, ''inasmuch as all the modes of Mind are modes of consciousness.''

''Let us, then, be convinced of this thing,'' said Monk, ''that greatness of mind consists in a great faculty of perceiving facts, and in nothing else; so that, if Napoleon was a great general, his greatness consisted in this — that he, facing the opposing general, more perceived the facts than the other? And if men are great enough to fly in our time, their greatness consists in this, that they perceive more facts than Icarus? And when they grow great to soar to Uranus, and to goad gold into uranium, their greatness will consist in a perception of facts, in a growth of consciousness? And, meantime, each of the boons that rebukes the hope of human or brute, each punishment which we stumble on, or bread of rueing which we bedrench and chew, is due to a defect of perception, a lack of consciousness of facts? Let us be convinced of this. But now, tell me: the things that present themselves to Mind as facts, are they not of two kinds? true and untrue?''

''That is so,'' I said.

''So that greatness of mind, which consists in perceiving facts, consists in perceiving the untruth of the untrue? and the truth of the true? Is this so?''

''That must be so,'' I agreed.

''So that greatness of mind consists in these two: (1) Scepticism, and (2) Proneness to truth — on the understanding that, though we call them two, yet they are but two phases, or faces, of the same one quality of Mind, namely, the faculty of perceiving facts? — of perceiving the untruth of the untrue, which we call scepticism? and of perceiving the truth of the true, which we call proneness? Is that so? And since the negative, scepticism, and the positive, proneness, are but two phases, or faces, of the same golden louis, must not the scepticism of any mind be an *exact* measure, or mirror, of its proneness to truth, as its proneness to truth must be an *exact* measure, or mirror, of its scepticism? as we see in savages and children, who have *exactly* so little proneness as they have little scepticism? and in philosophers, who have *exactly* so much proneness as they have much scepticism? Is all this sure, Shiel?''

"All this certainly seems to be so," I conceded.

"But as to Caesar," said Monk. "My business is to prove to you that there is scarce today a schoolboy in England who is not more sceptical, that is, who has not a greater proneness to truth, and faculty of perceiving facts, that is, who is not a greater mind, than Caesar. But have you, my friend, a *Gallic War* at hand that you could lend me?"

"I have," I answered, and ran and got it.

"I only hope that I shall be able quickly to find one of the passages which I have in my mind," muttered Monk, rushing through the pages, but he quickly found something, and begged me to read it aloud, since his eyes that night were sick.

In the passage — which I translate — Caesar is describing (from hearsay) certain German things, and he says: "In it (the Hercynian Forest) are many species of beasts which are not seen in other places, of which the most memorable are as follows: —

" 'There is a bull that has a stag's figure, from the middle of whose forehead, between the ears, one horn sticks up, taller and straighter than any horns known to *us;* and from its top, like palms, branches arch out. The nature of the male and female is the same, the same shape and size of horn.

" 'There are also some beasts called elks. These resemble he-goats in figure and coloring, and they have legs without any joints in them, so do not lie down to rest, nor, if by any chance they fall down, can they get up again. Tree-trunks serve as beds for these creatures; on tree-trunks they prop themselves, and so, only a little leaning, take their rest. And when huntsmen discover their haunts from their footprints, they cut through the trees thereabouts so much as to leave a semblance of trees still standing; then when the elks come and lean on the trees as usual, the elks' weights break the weakened trees, the elks tumble with the trees. (And, as they cannot get up again, the hunters come and take them so.)'''

"But, my friend," said Monk, when I had read it, "is this thing true, that there were such bulls and elks in the Hercynian Forest?"

"No," I said.

He leaned forward sharply, asking, *"How do you know?"*

"I do not trouble to ask myself how I know," I answered, "I only know that I know."

"But as to a Lancing lad," he said, "one who has no special knowledge as to elks; if one were to tell him this thing as to elks, is it not certain what he would say? Would he not murmur, 'draw it mild'?"

"Μάλιστά γε," I replied. "The boy would certainly employ words of such a kind."

"And is not this a fact like Cotopaxi," said Monk, "that statements about the cosmos that to a Lancing lad seem comic Caesar solemnly swallowed, and did not wink? Shall we not say that God has been jogging men? and that there appears here such a growth in scepticism, in general intelligence, or proneness to truth, that is, in greatness of mind — such a growth — for we laugh at Caesar in the same tone in which we laugh at infants and monkeys, without troubling to ask ourselves how we know the untruth of his statements — so great a growth, that Caesar and the people of his time must be defined as lower types of mind and life, we being somewhat to them as they to Bushmen, one stage above apes? and that it is beneath the dignity of modern men of your kind any longer to speak of suchlike types of life as 'great,' even though we still permit ourselves to ape their apish pages of legislation and foolish institutions? Of course, with a machine-gun under cover, one Rugby fag would easily have smashed ten-thousand tenth legions, generalled by ten-thousand Caesars; with one gunboat grumbling a Rugby brogue would have rolled up many Roman empires; and by the Roman world would certainly have been worshipped as that which he is, Mercury come with thunders from the pinnacles of Olympus. But that is not what I wished to show, but this, that, without the gun or the gunboat — though it is not fair, mind, to take the boat from the boy, since the boat is proper to him; he invented it, he or his uncle, or cousin; and Caesar would eagerly have invented it, if great enough; though, if he had attempted it, God would have mocked him, would not have cashed his check, since he would have been seeking to perceive truths of the universe proper to a higher type of life than his. Still, take the boat from the boy: then, I say that our boy, by his scepticism and proneness to truth, is of so far higher a type of mind and life than Caesar, that he would not have failed to prove himself in every respect as superhuman compared with Caesar. Or do you need me to adduce more proof of this?''

''No,'' I said, ''for one proof of a thing, if it be a sure proof, is enough; and no more is needed.''

''Very good,'' he said, ''but if the mind of Caesar was of this kind as compared with Rugby lads, how was it as compared with Spencer's or Kelvin's?''

''It was of a very much lower evolution,'' I said.

''And so, by definition, a savage?''

''Yes,'' I said.

"But as to Mr. Bernard Shaw," he said: "is he a savage?"

"Why, no," I answered.

"But do you know whether that is true what has been told me, that this Mr. Shaw has published the criticism that he is the best mind of our time?"

"I do not know if it is true," I replied, "but I, too, have been told by a friend that he has published this criticism."

"And if it is true that he has done so, is it not a savage criticism?" asked Monk.

"I think it a fatuous criticism," I answered; "but I confess I do not see why you call it savage."

"Let us consider it," said Monk. "Since the trait of mind is consciousness, or the preception of facts, then the signal of a *great* mind will be this, will it not, that it will perceive new facts — at any rate, some one fact that other minds have not contrived to perceive? Will not this be the signal of a great mind?"

"It cannot but be so," I assented.

"But as to Mr. Shaw: has he, then, perceived something new of the universe that you know of, that was not of the surface and froth of things?"

"No," I said.

"Has Mr. H. G. Wells?"

"Is it not he who has 'discovered the future'?" I said.

"A new discovery?"

"No," I said, "since it lay subconscious in all men and conscious in some; but still something of a discovery — with an assault, a consciousness, a largeness of thought, which were novel. Let us stretch a little, and give credit to fiction-writers, for if other men have a thought, that is not surprising; but if a fiction-writer has a thought, it is surprising; since fiction-writers have been such a tiny tribe.''

"That is very much so," said Monk. "But do you, then, a critic of intellects, as of machines which perceive facts, place Mr. Wells on a level with, or above, or below Mr. Shaw?''

"Above," I said.

"A little above? or well above?''

"Well above.''

"But are you sure, my friend, of this?''

"There is very little possibility of error," I said, "in the judgments of critics on suchlike things.''

"Let it be so, then," he said. "But as to Signor Marconi: tell me: has he perceived something new of the universe?''

"Yes," I said, "or wondrously nigh to new, and more things than one, be sure.''

"And do you as a critic of intellects place Mr. Wells on a level with him, or above, or below?''

"Below," I said.

"A little below? or well below?''

"Well below.''

"To me, too," he said, "what you say seems to be very much so: for, oh, my friend—we know his face—what a very temple and sacred place is that man's cranium wherein his Creator has elected to make his dwelling-place. How grandly it ramps and carries its ramparts, looking nearly as noble as it is — the brow of Caesar crowded with a thousand Caesar's crowns. Believe me, Shiel, nearly everything that it thinks is as true and sacred as nearly everything that the skulls of other men think is untrue and profane. But since some are well above Mr. Shaw, and those some well below other some, how wild appears this criticism of Mr. Shaw that he is above all.''

'' 'Wild,' if you like,'' I said, ''but you said 'savage.' ''

''But are not the criticisms of savages and children wild?'' he asked; ''and this criticism in particular, is it not rich in a certain skittishness, due to an unconsciousness of facts? in a certain kicking up of the heels, for one's own part, at the vague universe? rich, too, in its childish or savage over-belief?''

''I see the skittishness,'' I said, ''but not quite the over-belief.''

''Is it not *over*-believing,'' said Monk—''that is, *super*-stitious, *aber*-glaubig—because, like the over-beliefs of savages, it is a fantasy built upon fact? built upon a consciousness in Mr. Shaw of some actual intellectual energy? just as the over-belief of negroes that the corpse is hurrying home is built upon an actual quickening of the pace of the funeral? in each case a large and fantastic conclusion being elaborated on a puny basis of fact? And is not this savage?''

''True,'' I said. ''Nevertheless, let us look at it with some sweetness and light ——''

''Ah!'' he cried: ''but think, Shiel, of sticking the sweetness before the light, the cheap before the topaz of Ethiopia! And they are not the very best of friends! for light has a rather unsweet way of giving darkness warning to quit.''

''Then,'' said I, ''I will say with some humor. Mr. Shaw is a *farceur!* and his statements do not necessarily represent his beliefs. Even when he is serious beneath his farce, all the same, unknown to him, there is a lower and lowest stratum of farce beneath his seriousness: and this is skittish, but not, so to say, if I am a critic, skittishness of *intellect*. As to 'credulity,' he is truly sceptical; and if he has perceived no new fact, he has perceived many facts previously perceived by others; and that with much clearness and consciousness. Besides, one lie does not make a liar, nor one savage statement a savage — unless, indeed, it be such a statement as Caesar made as to elks, proving a furiously unsceptical stage of mental evolution.''

''Let it, then, be as you say,'' answered Monk. ''Besides, I am not blind to the fact that Mr. Shaw is partly to be pardoned in this, because of the now chronic rawness of the estimate that the feeble folk of art-writers, and artists in general, have formed of themselves, an estimate in which they cannot help being propped by the babbling and rawness of the populace. Curious fatuity! But how well would it be for the world if it could recognize its great men, and would stop erecting monuments to its petty men, who tickle it with pleasant little pictures and plays, tales and ditties. Baron Tennyson lies smiling with himself in Westminster Abbey, but try to find in *In Memoriam,* which moans to be thoughtful, a thought that was not some other man's thought; so that there is today many a mechanic gaining four pounds a week in motor-works and elsewhere of greater mind than the Baron, but will not be buried in the Abbey, nor, I think, will Marconi, causing all the gods and even geese to mock at our Simple-Simon simplicity. For that is rather true of art-writers, so far, what Socrates said: 'Taking up, therefore, some of their poems that appeared the most elaborately written, I asked what was their meaning, that I might learn something of them; and I am ashamed, indeed, O Athenians, to tell you the truth; for I discovered in a short time concerning the poets that they did not effect by wisdom that which they did, but by a certain enthusiastic energy, like prophets, and those that utter oracles; and at the same time I perceived that they considered themselves, on account of their poetry, to be the wisest of men in other things, in which they were not so.' So Socrates — and you yourself, I perceive, Shiel, will occasionally pen pleasant tales possessing no particular pressure of philosophy that I can see, of reason to be written, save their pleasantness, and this with wise titles and a certain bravura and burden, as though, forsooth, you were parturient with news of the universe: which is well for King's-jesters and artistes, but a little beneath the dignity, I conceive, of gifted intellects. Thus much, at any rate, as to Mr. Shaw. But as to Dante — was he a savage?''

''I have such a fondness,'' I began to say, ''for that *di parlar si largo fiume* ——''

''I also,'' said Monk; ''but my question was not as to amiability of Dante, but as to whether Dante was a savage, that is, whether he had far less scepticism and far less proneness to truth, than high minds. Did not Dante believe, and crib, everything that anybody ever said?''

''Why, no, he once differed from Aristotle,'' I answered.

''Ah! I did not know that. But you know, do you, that the whole scheme of the Inferno is based on a misunderstanding by Cicero of something that Aristotle said? that, in fact, a thing had only to get itself written in a book, and Dante took it for 'learning,' as every child does, and accepted it as certain — as when someone writes that lightning is a swift wind that gets ignited by friction, Dante gives that as his discovery, never asking himself whence the wind comes, or how it gets ignited, or why, being ignited, it does not fire everything? but, since the brain then had not the strength, the practice, the nimbleness, to think of several explanations, and select the best, catching, as all savages do, at the first explanation of a thing, triumphing in any explanation, and resting on that as on a prop, to prop his wee weak top, as children in learning to walk catch at the first thing? Is this a truth as to every page that Dante wrote? For I know that you know Dante in rather an expert way."

"Yes," I said, "all this is true as to Dante."

"Why, then," he asked, "did you say at first that Dante was not a savage?"

"Because," I answered, "I had not then clearly before my mind what a savage is; and because Dante was, after all, such a great poet."

"But not a great mind?"

"Well, no."

"So, then, you can have a great poet who is not a great mind? With what, then, does he write his poetry, if not with his mind? You can have a great wrestler, a great singer. But do not these do their feats with something else than their mind? Is this the case with a poet?"

"No," I said.

"Do you say, then, that Dante was not a great poet, since he was of weak mind?"

"Yes, I say so now," I said; and I added, "I should not have used the word 'great,' but should have said what I meant — a pleasant, a delicious, poet — pure water from the muses' well, I think."

"There I agree with you," Monk said, "though he was not *often* a delicious poet, either; for a poet who begins his verses with 'Oh, predestination!' is often apt to pen the opposite of poetry. Certainly, Beatrice was the dullest young woman that ever flew from star to star. With admirable artifice one is led to expect her all through the Inferno and Purgatorio, but when the girl does turn up, how great is her bathos! 'I will now treat this subject,' she says — *tratterò* — a stock word of the scholastics — and when she starts to treat, ah! who shall stop her? It is not merely that her treatings are empty of verity, but that they are empty of relevance, babblings whose fantasticalities lack any bearing, the most baby-like, the most brainless, on actualities; as when she explains to Dante in a prolonged 'treating' that the spots on the moon are not due to 'rare and dense,' as people 'down below' believed, but to an unequal diffusion of the Divine Virtù; for, since the moon was to Dante only a luminous mist, through which bodies could pass, the thought was *far* from cropping up in such a top as his that her spots might be owing to broken surfaces, though 1,700 years before it had occurred to Socrates that the moon might be a mass of earth: and I think that among the most comic things I see in the cosmos is the bringing out of new editions of such old authors *'With Notes'* and solemn comments on their pratings by modern ratepayers, the Rev. Philip Wicksteed, and other solemn *scholars* and unjesting gentlemen. As to his pretty trick of expression, I think with you that there are the very prettiest ripples of poetry when he stops being philosophic; but it must be said that the task that he set himself in harmony was far too hard for him, for the three rhymes in each triplet are not simple rhymes like cook, took, look, but double rhymes like summer, mummer, hummer — far too hard; so that he is hardly ever saying what he is impelled to say, but what he is compelled to say. And he is nearly always being philosophic — such philosophy! as though something could come out of nothing.''

"What precisely do you mean by this?" I asked — "'something coming out of nothing'?"

"But, my friend," said Monk, "can one think well under laughing-gas? or chloroform? To think at all one must be conscious?"

"Yes," I said.

"And consciousness is a knowledge of facts?"

"Quite so," I said.

"So, without a knowledge of facts, thought is impossible?"

"I see that," I said.

"Do you say, then, that thought was a new thing on earth in the nineteenth century, since knowledge was a new thing? And that it was quite in vain for the ancients to sit down and think hard about things, as savages and apes do, without having any knowledge of anything?"

"Yes, if knowledge, as you say, was a new thing in the nineteenth century."

"Practically, was it not?" said Monk. "It is impossible to know anything, except by experiment! for if you go guessing you are perfectly certain to guess all over the place; and experiment, roughly speaking, was a nineteenth century thing? As to such a man as Dante, it may be said that he knew nothing. He knew that the sky looks blue, and he knew some Euclid, and the names of the constellations. The rest of his 'learning' consisted in having at his finger-ends a string of Greek myths, which was not knowledge — not knowledge of things, BE-ing, I AM — and never could a little help him to think. We two here, do we not owe the whole tone of our souls to the recent discovery that the universe is no nook? But Dante's universe, the cosy human home! of which a human female was the queen.

For although his sun was but a lamp and planet of the earth, all his stars shone by that tiny sun's shine, though, ages before, Philolaus and some Pythagoreans had had the notion that our globe might be rolling round a sun which was the center of everything. Nor was this toy-universe filled by his God! 'O our Father, who stayest in Heaven,' he says — 'in Heaven, not because Thou art circumscribed, but because of the greater love which Thou hast for the first-created beings up there.' And notice that facility — so deliciously characteristic of children — with which his intellect accepts both of two contradictory concepts. He has heard it said that 'God is not circumscribed'; and he has heard it said that God is circumscribed by the greater love which He has for the first-created beings up there, compelling Him to live up there. He believes both — *easily,* and does not one bit care whether in the same phrase he says that God is not circumscribed, and that God is circumscribed. And I say, let modern men continue to revel in the pretty tricks of expression of suchlike types of life, but let no modern man — if he *is* genuinely modern — if he has diligently made himself worthy to be called by that name whereby the lords of the earth are called — let him not in reading these people read them as equals, nor any longer deign to give to them the name of 'great,' since that is beneath his dignity, and indeed, ungodly. Enough, however, as to Dante. But as to Milton: Is Milton still not a savage?''

"We will now say of Milton that he was a savage," I said.

"Yes, but have you reflected how essentially a savage, my friend?" asked Monk. "Do you recall to yourself that Milton lived definitely in the dawn of the day of Revelation? Thirty years or so (my dates may be shaky) before his birth Copernicus had closed his eyes, holding that Holy Book that he had indited in his hand. Little Milton cared. By the date of his birth, Galileo had discovered the isochronism of the pendulum, had proved that all bodies fall with an equal velocity, had invented the water-thermometer, and with his new optic tube had noted the moons of Jupiter, the ansated form of Saturn, the spots on the sun, the phases of Venus. I think that before Milton was a lad, Kepler must have published his *Three Laws;* and when Milton, a young man, called upon Galileo, an old man, in Italy, Galileo had given out his *Dialoghi delle nuove Scienze.* And let Milton's proneness to truth be estimated by the fact that in this new activity of intellect he not only had no part, but it did not a little dig the nigger to any tingling. The cosmography in *Paradise Lost* is Ptolemaic! because it was Ptolemaic in the *Divine Comedy* — as if Milton had never *heard* of Copernicus. One of the things which I can never understand is how all savages did not always see that our globe goes about the sun, an inability I can no more sympathize with than they grasp Grotthüs's doctrine of travelling hydrogen in electrolysis, or the flashes of light on which we fly: they are to be forgiven for this, as I am to be forgiven for not seeing myriads of things on the face of nature that men will yet see: but how great must be the negro grain of a being, who, when the thing which he cannot see for himself has been seen for him by seers, and revealed to him, receives God's holy truth with indifference or unbelief, with a top preoccupied with Greek and negro crotchets and the resurrection of the dead, clinging to night, and for some motive or other liking it more than light!''

''I see that what you say of Milton is true,'' I said, ''though he is my favorite poet.''

"Mine are Job and Lucretius," said Monk, "and I think that Milton comes next for me . . . I love his pretty trick of expression, and his *os magna sonans,* and I love children and negroes. But I don't love unconsciousness in grown-up Circassians. And is it not a thing very ridiculous that unsceptical critics should still in our day be teaching the people in their reading to say of suchlike types of life, not 'ah, how agreeable,' but 'ah, how great'? But so it will continue to be, until the government begins to give to the citizen an education intimate with things, BE-ing, I AM, and not with myths. Myths and Milton were intimates! his ambition being to beat the poor Dante (who could not read Greek), in having at his finger-ends a string of Greek and Biblical things, his knowledge of which he was more eager to exhibit than to give ear to the things of God, that His elect were then investigating: so that about the time when Huygens was adapting the pendulum to the clock, when Torricelli was weighing the air, when Mariotte was discovering the law of pressure, and Römer the velocity of light, and von Guericke was making an air-pump,* we find the schoolman-mind of Milton proving his proneness to truth by pouring forth polemics on church-government and the resurrection of the body; yes, and just when he was whirling out a world of such words as 'Hail, holy light, offspring of heaven first-born,' Newton was writing this: 'When I understood this I left off my aforesaid Glassworks: for I saw that telescopes were limited, not so much for want of glass, as because that *Light itself is a heterogeneous mixture of differently refrangible rays.*' Think of the interval betwixt these intellects, in quiddity and quantity,

---

* And Papin a steam-boat!

the chasm! Think of 'offspring of heaven first-born'! He saw candles: and he saw light: and he saw candles that did not give out any light, but he never saw light that was not given out by candles, or by some kind of matter: should not the littlest infant's intellect instantly pitch to the decision that light must be the child of some passion of matter? that matter must antedate light? that candlelight cannot exist without a candle? or sunlight without a sun? But he had heard that somebody had asserted that light was 'first-born ("let there be light!"),' and his wee weak top, that caught at all things as a prop, was so blocked up and preoccupied with showing off his knowledge of a hotchpotch of such borrowed crotchets, as the black of Congoland cocks a battered top-hat on his head, and, naked else, rakishly promenades so arranged to parade his charm, that such a thing as thinking was as distant as Wittiput from his sinciput. Shall we say, then, that Milton was a savage, not as compared with high minds, but as compared with Newton?"

"We shall say so," I said. "But was not Newton, then, one of the high minds? Or are we to say that Newton, too, was something of a savage?"

"But, my friend, is that not certainly so?" asked Monk. "Supposing that Copernicus and Kepler, Galileo and Newton had not made their investigations, and supposing that, nevertheless, the mind of man had gone on evolving as it did — though that's impossible — then, is it not certain that at the birth of the nineteenth century a million minds in Europe and America would instantly have leapt to the discoveries of those splendid fellows? They are not, to tell the truth, very abstruse. And since the discoveries that appeared to them enormous appears to us small and obvious, shall we not say that they were rather savages? Let us say this, then, with respect to Newton as compared with Kelvin and Edison, though we say it with our heads bent, as to no other savage.''

''Let it be so, then,'' said I: ''but as to poets, and that beauty of theirs which you admit, but despise, think how great in usefulness, Monk!''

''That *I* despise?'' replied Monk: ''but, my friend, I do nothing of this kind, since I well descry the truth that that beauty of poets is more useful than wireless; nay, that it is the fruit of a true perception in poets: for, in truth, perception, if empty of emotion, of the mood of music, the flush of love, and stress of Eros, is perception pale and lame, like electricity stricken sick if empty of potential. As a matter of fact, Hertzian waves are wonderful and Divine: and to whatever extent Marconi's perception of them is empty of a Divine piety and emotion of wonder, empty of that baby amaze of Job and cat's abstraction staring at the staring moon in a universe new-made that day, to that extent must his perception of Hertzian waves be inert and imperfect. In this respect, then, poets, painters, tale-tellers have been true perceivers, for they have perceived (*what* they have perceived — the moon moving, human moods and dooms, etc.) in an emotional or impassioned manner; and Socrates was wrong in assuming that their 'enthusiasm' is not 'wisdom' for it is the quiddity of wisdom, is true, and has proved most useful in seducing mankind to view the universe in this manner. So that a critic would not, in strict truth, degrade words in asserting that one poet or painter has been *'greater'* than another, since these have been true perceivers, and even new feelers; but will he not degrade words in asserting that some one of them has been *'great'* because beautiful and useful, although some of the most beautiful and useful, and newest feelers, have been known as people of feeble or sick intellects, idiots nearly, as Turner, Tasso, Scott, and a multitude more? For, at that rate, if greatness were in beauty and usefulness, the very greatest of men would be perfumers, dyers, miners: but as Plutarch observes, 'we are pleased with purples and perfumes, but look upon dyers and perfumers as mean mechanics.' Not therefore in beauty or usefulness is the grain of greatness, but in the depth of perception — the scepticism and proneness to truth — represented in anything. Or has this not already been proved by us?''

''Yes,'' I said, ''that has been proved.''

''But as to Plato of Athens,'' he said, ''is he still not a savage?''

''Truth to tell,'' I said, ''I still find it difficult to think of Plato as a savage; so much so that if the definition makes him a savage, I shall be inclined to suspect the definition of error somewhere.''

''But shall we not be reasonable?'' asked Monk: ''Is not the definition the outcome of reasoning?''

''Yes, certainly,'' I said.

''But your notion that Plato was not a savage, is it not the outcome of something else than reasoning? Has a habitual assumption, and a college prejudice, nothing to do with it?''

''That, too, is no doubt true.''

''And though reasoning is not a good guide to truth, will you not say that it is the least bad that we have when based on knowledge? and less bad than habitual assumption or prejudice?''

''I will say so, Monk.''

''So, then,'' he said, ''if the definition clashes with your notion that Plato was not a savage, will you properly begin to think the definition wrong, which is the outcome of reasoning, or will you properly begin to think your notion wrong that Plato was not a savage, which is the outcome of habitual assumption? or will you incline to slight your less bad guide to follow your worse?''

''No,'' I meekly said, ''I will rather choose to cling to my least bad guide than to my worst. But was Plato, then, a savage by the definition?''

''But had not Plato a skittish, credulous, over-believing mind in comparison with high minds?''

''Tell me of it!'' I said.

''But was Plato not a member of a society that condemned Socrates to die because Socrates had taught the doctrine that the sun is not a god, but a stone? Is this Congoland? Or how say you? And if you reflect how very far that handful of savages are said to have surpassed us in the arts, as the Japanese also are thought to do, you will the deeper agree with the truth of my statement that greatness of mind is in no relation with the producing of pretty things, but with perception of truth, and that savages may be, and are, charming artists. Consider also how fantastic to farce, and far from the reality, are the mirages which the average don, or such fantastic doctors as Ruskin, have fashioned in their skulls of that handful of savages. Certainly, very worthy representatives of that handful of savages were Euclid and Aristotle — and Plato, too, in his way: but Newton in his youth refused to bother to con Euclid, whose truths were too obvious to him; and, of course, a modern schoolboy every night at prep spryly romps through five 'riders' five times abstruser than Euclid ever brooded on — Euclid, or Archimedes, or Hiero, or Ctesebius — and darted from their baths to scream through the streets: *'eureka!'* As to Plato and his thinkings, could something come out of nothing? Can Mr. Lloyd George think without statistics? without experts, and actuaries, and specialists, and a knowledge of economy? And, if Plato chloroformed was little more unconscious than Plato un-chloroformed, could Plato unchloroformed think, though he might prettily play at thinking? Did Plato believe that all knowledge is but a remembering — in which case the ancients had bad memories — and a dozen other things of this sort? did he not make an attempt to prove by dialectics the immortality of the soul of mammals, himself believing in it?''

''He did.''

''But what were the grounds of this undoubting belief of Plato's and Cato's? Were they the kind of grounds whereon high minds found their undoubting beliefs? or were they the kind of grounds whereon negro tribes weakmindedly prop their undoubting belief in this same thesis, namely, the adumbrations and mirages of their brains, as when at a foot-funeral the pace smartens and the corpse is thought to be hurrying home? On the latter you will say? You can't imagine Signor Marconi, or even Sir Oliver Lodge, writing a book to prove by dialectics that the soul of animals is immortal?''

''No.''

''And is not this shyness of high minds about laying down the law as to the unknown the fruit of a growth of responsibility and exactitude, as when a grown-up lad casts aside his Wild-west romances? and enters seriously into business?''

''There is undoubtedly,'' I said, ''that growth of responsibility and exactitude among us.''

"But in this attempt to settle once for all the immortality of the soul by logic-chopping, does there not attach to Plato and Descartes a skittishness and unconsciousness, as of a filly frisking in spring, or as of the builders of Babel saying, 'come let us build to the moon, which is sometimes quite near above the tree-tops'?"

"I think I catch what you wish to point out," I answered.

"But," said Monk, "if Plato was thus superstitious and skittish as compared with us, was he not a savage, what though he attained the highest moral, sociable, and physical evolution of the historic ages?"

"This, too, I must admit," I answered.

"But if Plato, the charming, and Cato, the hard-headed, and Caesar *con gli occhi grifagin,* had childish minds, shall we not say that *all* the minds of former ages were likewise savage? and that only modern minds are not savage?"

"It does seem so," I said.

"But as to a navvy of Whitechapel who cannot read: do you still say that he is a savage?"

"Yes," I answered, "I still say so."

"But suppose, Shiel," said Monk, "that the man leads a moderately moral life, that he sometimes washes himself and attends to his nails, that he says, 'tank you kindly' when anything is done for him: is such a one *far* from the average of the historic ages in the moral, sociable, and physical respects?"

"No," I said, "but there remains the mental; he cannot read: he is far from the highest mental evolution of our age; his mind will have the notes of a child's."

"But are you sure that this is so?" asked Monk. "Let us look into it. We consented just now that scepticism is the bloom of mental evolution; but of what is mental evolution itself the bloom?''

"How do you mean?" I asked.

"Tell me this," he said: "in what does mental evolution manifest itself?"

"In a new and higher way of thinking," I answered.

"Just so. But did we not see that one does not think well under chloroform? That in order to think at all one must be conscious? that the more conscious one is, the better one thinks? and that consciousness is a knowledge of facts? so that the more we know of facts, the better we think, that is, the higher our mental evolution? Did we not consent to this?"

"Yes," I said.

"So is not mental evolution the bloom of an enlarged consciousness, the bloom of knowledge?"

"That is clearly so."

"And 'knowledge' and 'science' are words of the same meaning? the one being Saxon and the other Latin?"

"Yes."

"So mental evolution is the bloom of science? its manifestation being thinking in a certain scientific way?"

"That must be so," I said.

"And the mental evolution of the nineteenth century, its quite new and higher way of thinking, was it not the bloom of a great growth of knowledge, or science, or consciousness?"

"Undoubtedly."

"But, come now," he said: "did not Lord Kelvin know more than Lord Rosebery?"

"So I suppose," I answered.

"Yet is not Lord K.'s and Lord R.'s modern way of thinking,

that is, their mental evolution, about the same, even though mental evolution is the bloom of science, and Lord K. has the more science?''

''That is so,'' I answered.

''How, then, do you account for this?'' he asked.

''It can only be,'' I answered, ''that all knowledge, or science, has not an equal virtue in evolving the mind and heightening its way of thinking, but that those particular facts of science which Lord K. and Lord R. have learned in common have some special virtue in this respect.''

''But, then,'' he said, ''those facts can't be many, since most of the facts known by Lord K. are of a very different sort from those known by Lord R.?''

''No,'' I said, ''I believe that they are even few.''

''But, surely, since they are few, and since their effect upon the mind is so mighty, must it not be that they make up in splendor and large-mindedness for what they lack in number?''

''It must be so,'' I agreed.

''But, in that case, since they are few and large, you and I, as modern people, know and can repeat them off-hand: are they not these: that the nearest sun is a good many millions of millions of leagues distant? that our globe, though far, far vaster than all mortal thought — as the Isle of Wight is — is but a spattering of matter in comparison with our sun, which, nevertheless, is among the littlest of many millions of suns? that all things are changing? and changing in their sum for the better? that man is a cousin to monkeys and dogs? that living things appeared on our globe millions of eras ago? and, growing ever more knowing and august, will, without doubt, continue on it for millions of aeons to come? and some others of this vast-minded simple sort?''

"Yes," I said, "it can only be the consciousness of such truths as these that causes the new way of thinking of both Lord Rosebery and Lord Kelvin."

"But, come," said Monk: "may not our navvy have come to know these facts in a hundred ways, even though he cannot read? May he not, besides, have pondered them in his head on his bed at night, and accepted them into his constant consciousness? And, having known the truth, shall not the truth make him free? so educating and evolving him, that he thenceforth thinks of the cosmos in a well-grown, scientific, sceptical way, and is a good deal less weak to lean upon any queer thing that he hears or fancies of the universe than Basutos are, or than Dante was? And since the further facts learned by Lord Kelvin are so like nothing in comparison with those large-minded ones, that Lord Rosebery has still somewhat the same mental evolution as Lord K., are not the further facts learned by Lord R. so like nothing, that the navvy may still have somewhat the same mental evolution as Lord R.? But he must be *far* from having this, in order to be a savage. Do you still say, then, that such a navvy is a savage?"

"No," I answered, "for I see now that he is by no means a savage."

"But as to Cardinal Newman," said Monk: "do you still say that he was not a savage?"

"But was not Newman, then, a modern man?" I said: "Did he not know all those large-minded facts by the knowledge of which Lord K., Lord R., and our navvy are not savages?"

"But we did not say that by the knowledge of them they are not savages," said Monk, "but we said that by the knowledge of them their minds have evolved, and by the evolution of their minds they are not savages. Is that not so?"

"True," I answered.

"Is it not a matter of common comment," said Monk, "that knowledge does not invariably evolve the brain, as in the case of the average graduate, and grallae crammed for exams? In order that knowledge may effect this, must it not somehow digest itself into consciousness, since knowledge and consciousness are not exactly one thing, but consciousness is knowledge in action? Must not one, then, picture the objects of knowledge to oneself, feeding upon them in the heart, and becoming instantly conscious of them, in order that they may make us better men? And if these large-minded facts, which, once taken into the heart, infallibly save a man from kiddishness, still left the Cardinal skittish, credulous, over-believing, and stubborn, what shall be said of him? Shall we not say that through some kiddish stubbornness, or other reason, having ears, he did not hear? but skittishly kicked up his heels at the truth? and, knowing the truth, retained the unconsciousness of a savage?"

"Yes," I consented, "we shall say this of him, if only you are able to show that he did remain skittish, credulous, over-believing, and stubborn, in despite of light and knowledge."

"But how shall I be able to show this, Shiel," said Monk, "except by appealing to your general sense of Newman's intellect? Unless, indeed, you have something written by him at hand among your books?"

"I have all his writings," I replied, "for I have a liking for his style."

"I, too," said Monk. "But bring some book of his at haphazard, and, opening at random, read where your eye happens to light."

On this I rose, got the *Apologia,* and coming again to Monk, read the following: "'I used (when a boy) to wish the Arabian tales were true; my imagination ran on unknown influences, on magical powers and talismans; I thought life might be a dream, or I an angel, and all this world a deception, my fellow-angels by a playful device concealing themselves from me, and deceiving me with the semblance of a material world. . . . When I was fifteen (in the autumn of 1816) a great change of thought took place in me. I fell under the influence of a definite creed, and received into my intellect impressions of dogma, which, through God's mercy, have never been affected or obscured.'''

"Well, that was the boy," said Monk when I stopped; "and how unsoiled, how blameless a boy, though spoiled, and pale! I would only remark as to the passage in general a certain grab as of the crab's claw with which early notions, through God's mercy, took hold upon his consciousness, as one sees it at its acme in Methodist and Catholic negroes: a grasp and grimness which once forced from his lips the opinion that heretics should be shown no pity."

"No, not 'heretics,'" I said, "'heresiarchs'; I believe I can even discover the passage" — and after a hunt I discovered and read: "'the latter (any ''heresiarch'') should meet with no mercy; to spare him is a false and dangerous pity. . . . I cannot deny,' he continues, 'that this is a very fierce passage, but it is only fair to myself to say that neither at this nor at any other time of my life, not even when I was fiercest, could I have even cut off a Puritan's ears, and I think the sight of a Spanish *auto-da-fé* would have been the death of me. Again, when one of my friends wrote to expostulate with me on the course I was taking, I said that we would ride over him and his as Othniel prevailed over Chusan-rishathaim, King of Mesopotamia ——'''

"Oh, well, let that pass," said Monk, interrupting me, "since no comment is necessary. With regard, by the way, to 'Othniel prevailing over Chusan-rishathaim,' this is a very negro thing, the referring of modern cases to Biblical ones, and finding likenesses between them. This of 'Othniel' is not a good instance, for it is semi-humorous, I think: but Newman was given to it. It is over-belief gone doting! as when any sudden death in Barbados will instantly bring to many a lip the words 'Ananias and Sapphira.' Newman, I remember, once drew an elaborate analogy between the seceding Ten Tribes and the Church of England, in order to show that, *as* the ten tribes were still recognized as a people 'by the divine mercy,' and *as* the Shunamite 'received no command' to break off from her own people, *therefore* there is no call for an Anglican to leave his church for Rome. As to the rest of the passage which you have read, let nothing be said. The cutting off of a Puritan's ears, or a Spanish *auto-da-fé,* would have been the death of Newman, solely because of his very advanced moral evolution; as to the mentality of the whole thing, is it not a skittish and irrelevant piece of scripture to proceed from a modern pen? Fierce also and stubborn? Childish, then, and savage? You will say that this is so. But that is a mere straw, showing possibly which way the wind blows. Read something else somewhere."

I turned some pages and met the passage: "'It is Milner's doctrine that upon the visible Church came down from above, at certain intervals, large and temporary *effusions* of divine grace. In a note he adds that "in the term *effusion* there is *not* here included the idea of the miraculous operations of the Spirit"; but still it was natural for me, admitting Milner's theory, not to stop short at his abrupt *ipse dixit,* but boldly to pass forward to the conclusion that, as miracles accompanied the first effusion of grace, so they might accompany the latter, and that there was no force in the popular argument that, because we did not see miracles with our own eyes, miracles were not taking place in distant places. . . .'''

''Notice,'' said Monk, ''the somehow lovable skittishness — the half self-conscious skittishness — of 'distant places'; the kicking up of the heels, for one's own part, at the vague universe! Must it not have entered his head, even as he said it, that there are no more any *distant places* since the coming of steam, except in Thibet, and Caesar's 'Hercynian Forest,' for miracles to take place in? But little he recked! and with tight eyes frisked from behind, executing mentally that back-kick of the cake-walk. Unless, indeed, he meant 'distant places,' not here beneath, but on, say, the nearest star? And yet, hardly on this, I think, for the nearest star seems never to have got well into Newman's consciousness, no more than steam fully got, inasmuch as in his youth mail-coaches crawled, and his youth, as he relates, remained always with him. But this passage is so much less modern than anything in Aristotle! So read something else.''

At this I turned over, and lighted upon the following: '''It was, I suppose, to the Alexandrian school and to the early Church that I owe what I definitely held about the angels. I viewed them as carrying on the economy of the visible world. This doctrine I have drawn out in my sermon for Michaelmas Day, written in 1831. I say of the angels, ''Every breath of air and ray of light and heat, every beautiful prospect is, as it were, the skirts of their garments, the waving of the robes of those whose faces see God.'' Again, I ask what would be the thoughts of a man who, ''when examining a flower or a pebble, suddenly discovered that he was in the presence of some powerful being who was hidden behind the visible things he was inspecting, whose robe and ornaments these objects were?'' Also, besides the hosts of evil spirits, I considered there was a middle race, δαιμόνια, neither in heaven nor in hell; partially fallen, capricious, wayward; noble or crafty, benevolent or malicious, as the case might be. In 1837 I made a further development of this doctrine ——' ''

''A *further* development?'' said Monk at this point — '' 'in 1837'?''

''Let me finish,'' I said; and I read on: '' 'In 1837 I made a further development of this doctrine. I said to a dear friend, Samuel Francis Wood, in a letter: I have an idea. The mass of the Fathers hold that, though Satan fell from the beginning, the angels fell before the Deluge, falling in love with the daughters of men. Daniel speaks as if each nation had its guardian-angel. I cannot but think that there are beings with a great deal of good in them, yet with great defects, who are the animating principles of certain institutions, etc., etc. . . . Take England with many high virtues, and yet a low Catholicism: it seems to me that John Bull is a spirit neither of heaven nor hell. . . .' ''

''Well,'' said Monk, ''all that seems to me skittish and over-believing. Does it not to you?''

''Well, yes,'' I consented.

''Observe,'' he said, ''that this is not mere fancy, but fancy accepted as authentic, and become *belief*. He does not say that every breath of air may be, 'as it were, the skirts of the angels' garments'; but he says that every breath *is*, as it were, that; and he is so confirmed that it is so, that he journeys forth, urging it, in a church, upon others, laying it down as a fact that so the matter stands on that particular 'Michaelmas Day.'''

"The fancy, though, is pretty," I said, "and full of that world-wonder which you love in Job."

"It is very prettily expressed, anyway in one sentence," he said, "much more prettily than in Dante and *Religio Medici,* where we have the fancy in all its details; but as to your reference, my friend, to Job, really I can't help thinking that here your criticism deeply sleeps. *Catch* Job puking such pap! Job, too, of course, is a child-mind — true: but a most robust country-child; Newman a most artificial child, a sophisticated, a sickly. Job's interest is all riveted on things BE-ing, I AM, on onyx, on coral, on spittle, on skin of teeth, on the number of the months, on Boötes, on stones, on wild asses' colts, on conies, on wild goats, on dust of gold, on all the manners and customs of this unrolling of the Glory of the Most High God, whose gonfalons roam on their road before his eyesight: so that he lacks the time to *care* whether there are angels roguishly ogling under stones, he is so ghast with marvelling at stones themselves, at sparks that fly upward, not sideward or otherward, with marvelling that there are sparks at all, or aught at all, and 'O,' he calls out, 'it is all as lofty as heaven, what can'st thou do? profounder down than hell, what can'st thou know?'' Newman, on the other hand, in his callousness, as to the actual marvel of stones, has to manufacture a fantastic marvel of angels roguishly ogling under stones, to make stones a little interesting to him, for since a marvel to interest him has to be grotesque, in things, BE-ing, I AM, he has no gram of interest, his interest is in I AM's son's mother and grandmother. Do not, then, be likening Newman with Job, but with Oscar Wilde: for these two Oxford-men, so dissimilar-looking, were, in truth, beings curiously alike in fibre to the eye of criticism, Newman being a kind of white-eyed Wilde, or Wilde-in-chokey adoring *Sorrow,* Newman, too, *roué,* luxurious, uxorious, pain his holy whore, not 'pleasure,' pain being his pleasure, but both men of the same mental measure, men made of mosaic, of paint and paste, infinitely artificial, fantastic, packed with padding to the pancreas, their pansies wallpaper pansies, their landscape a tapestry landscape, their sun a monstrance sun, all most aesthetically wrought! — or wrought in a way that they had heard someone say was aesthetic; and never the feet of either got down to God's grand grass and ragged ground. But as to the beauty of the fancy in question, does not a poet inform us with some plausibleness that 'beauty is truth, truth beauty'? If there be no truth in the fancy, perhaps there is no true beauty. But in its possible beauty or truth we are not at present interested: for, since believed in without experiment or grounds, even if it were beautiful, and by some chance true, must it not be regarded as still negroid, over-believing, obiahish? peopling the air with demons and semi-demons, and angels? of which semi-demons Plato tells us that 'through their intervention we possess every kind of divination and incantation, and the whole of magic'? investing the shapes of the fancy with a certain actualness and awe? and elaborating them with a certain precision and conviction? as some savages arranged Judgment Day on the apparition of a ship's flashlight? and as all children and savages do?''

''Yes, that certainly seems to be so,'' I said.

''But read something else,'' said Monk.

I turned over and read as follows: '' 'First was the principle of dogma: my battle was with liberalism; by liberalism I mean the anti-dogmatic principle. This was the first point on which I was certain. Here I make a remark: persistence in a given belief is no test of its truth; but departure from it is at least a slur upon the man who has felt so certain about it. From the age of fifteen dogma has been the fundamental principle of my religion: I know no other religion; I cannot enter into the idea of any other sort of religion. . . .'''

''But is not this yet another proof of mental stubbornness?'' demanded Monk.

''There is a certain stubbornness in it,'' I answered.

''Notice especially,'' he said, ''how remote Newman is from the modern mood where he says that departure from a given belief is 'a slur' upon the man who has felt so certain of it: for even in politics a total *volte-face* is no longer reckoned much; and can anything be nimbler than the ease wherewith scientific intellects again and again give up their beliefs, standing constantly brisk and prompt to give them up the moment that their own or another's discoveries prove them in some trifle unprecise?''

''That is very much so,'' I assented.

''But a Methodist negro would rather greet a martyr's death than incur 'the slur' of an altering of belief? this stubbornness being owing to the fact that what the savage loves is not so much truth as his own belief and *parti pris?* and a kind of feeling that he is necessarily right? and a biped better than anybody in the binding of his fibre?''

''I suppose that this, too, is so,'' I said, ''from what you have told me as to negroes.''

''And, on the whole,'' he said, ''with regard to the seeking after truth, does not the matter somehow stand somewhat in this wise: that man was made to seek after truth, but that in his childish or savage state he merely plays at seeking after it? in the childish-lovable manner of, for example, Sir Thomas Browne, or of Milton? and is skittish with respect to it, as children play at soldiers or at keeping store? but when time more matures man's mind, man enters seriously into business with respect to truth? and into real warfare because of it, in the way of a well-grown stripling? And as amid the games of children the passions gush out, with arrogances, and stubbornnesses, and personal wayward-nesses, like Achilles withdrawing into his tent (though the cause of the quarrel is of no consequence), but actual business and warfare is carried on with a certain earnest and impersonal calm for their own sake, so the savage is passionate, personal, and rooted in his playing at truth? and the controversies of the ages have been conducted with rages and stubbornness? like child's-play? . . . Imagine a controversy betwixt Milton and Newman! That would have been pleasant! 'Fierce as ten furies, terrible as hell' . . . ha, ha. Would not Milton have new-named Newman 'that pork'? and would not Newman have doomed Milton, deep, deep, even if he did not 'cut off his ears'? But scientific controversies are not so conducted? but with a well-grown calm? everyone standing brisk and prompt to give up his opinion for God's sake? and not thinking this any 'slur' on him? Does not the matter stand somewhat as I have stated it?''

''It seems to me to be even as you say,'' I answered.

''But read further,'' he said.

I turned the leaves, and read as follows: '''As a matter, then, of conscience, I felt it to be a duty to protest against the Church of Rome: for I adopted the argument of Bernard Gilpin that Protestants were not able to give any firm and solid reason of the separation besides this, to wit, that the Pope is antichrist. . . .'''

"Well, let that, too, pass," said Monk: "for all that one need remark is that it seems no more sceptical to believe that the good easy Pope is antichrist than to believe that a battleship's flashlight is antichrist; moreover, Newman abandoned his belief in his latter years, proving that, if he was as over-believing as, he was at least less stubborn than, a Methodist of Barbados, who *never* abandons it: so read further."

I again turned the leaves and read as follows: " 'Starting, then, with the being of a God I look out of myself into the world, and there I see a sight which fills me with distress. The world seems simply to give the lie to that great truth of which my whole being is so full. The sight of the world is nothing else than the prophet's scroll, "full of lamentations and mourning and woe." To consider it in its length and breadth, its various history, the tokens so faint and broken of a superintending design, the idolatries, the corruptions, the dreary hopeless irreligion, the condition of the whole race so fearfully, yet exactly, described in the Apostle's words, "having no hope and without God in the world" — all this is a vision to dizzy and appal; and inflicts upon the mind the sense of a mystery which is absolutely beyond human solution. . . .' "

"He prattles prettily," said Monk at this point, "and how prettily you read him aloud!"

"I will finish the passage," I said; and I continued to read: " 'What will be said of this reason-bewildering fact? I can only answer that either there is no Creator, or this society of men is in a true sense discarded from His presence. And so I argue about the world — *if* there be a God, *since* there is a God, the human race is implicated in some terrible aboriginal calamity. It is out of joint with the purposes of its Creator. And now, supposing it were the loving will of the Creator to interfere in this anarchical condition of things, what are we to suppose would be the methods which might be naturally involved in His purpose of Mercy? .... There is nothing to surprise the mind, if He should think fit to introduce a Power into the world invested with the prerogative of infallibility in religious matters; and when I find that this is the very claim of the Catholic Church, there is a fitness in it which recommends it to my mind. . . . The Church must denounce rebellion as of all possible evils the greatest; she must have no terms with it; if she would be true to her Master, she must ban and anathematize it. This is the meaning of a statement of mine which has furnished matter for one of those accusations to which I am replying: I said, 'The Catholic Church holds it better for the sun and the moon to drop from heaven, for the earth to fail, and for all the many millions on it to die of starvation in extremest agony, than that one soul should commit one single venial sin, should tell one wilful untruth.'''

"I think that in some respects he writes well," said Monk when I stopped, "though wordily. But as a matter of fact, is not this passage skittish, credulous, over-believing and, above all, stubborn?"

"In what particular points do you mean?" I asked.

"Let us glance at the argument," said Monk: "he first of all insists upon God's existence — a singular insistence, by the way, for did any living being ever question the fact that the order of things must have a cause of some sort, a cause which we English call 'God'? But the fact of the matter is, that it is not upon the existence of the infinite God, infinitely inconceivable, that Newman is insisting, but it is upon the existence of God as conceived by the geese-heads of Greeks and negroes, viz., as a living thing, that is, a mortal, yet immortal, an immortal mortal, a mammal or enormous tortoise inhabiting a habitat *lassù,* as Dante says, 'up there.' Anyway, God, he insists, exists; but the world is a denial of God's existence, 'the world is out of joint with the purposes of its Creator, through some terrible aboriginal calamity,' the fall of man in Eden; in which state of things, he says, it was natural that God should establish some fabric like the Catholic Church, infallible, claiming to be so, and proclaiming that 'it is better for the sun and moon to drop from heaven than that one soul should tell one untruth'; as to which one can't help pausing to remark on this irreverent way of talking of the sun and moon in the same breath — and *drop* where to? Upon Oxford probably? Could he have had Oxford in his mind, my friend?''

''As to that, I do not know what to think,'' I answered.

''But in that case,'' said Monk, ''would not the splash of the sun's dropping in especial spread even to Littlemore? making some derangement even there?''

''It would without doubt,'' I consented, ''spread even to Littlemore.''

''But does not the fact that he says 'the sun and moon,' and not 'the moon and sun' seem to show that he was at least subconscious that the sun is more than the moon?''

''He seems to have been at least subconscious of it,'' I answered.

''Suppose he had said 'the moon and sun'! That would have been pleasant! like 'sweetness and light' — the cart forty millions of millions of miles before the horse. But does not the fact that he babbles in this facile fashion in the same breath of 'the sun and moon' 'dropping' 'from heaven' upon Oxford or elsewhere indicate that he was not instantly conscious of the truth about the sun and about the moon, or, in general, of those large-minded truths by the evolving breath of which Lord Kelvin, Lord Rosebery, and our navvy of Whitechapel are no longer childish?''

''What you say does seem to have some likelihood,'' I answered.

''But to go back to his argument: he bases his faith in an infallible fabric upon 'the fall of man,' and if his premise is good, his conclusion may be good, too. But is it not so that his clinging to that premise was skittish, credulous, and, above all, stubborn?''

''Is that a provable thing?'' I asked.

''But is it not a provable thing,'' Monk demanded, ''that in a former age all Britons were savages?''

''Yes,'' I said.

''But we here are no longer so?''

''No.''

''So it is a provable thing that we here have evolved from lower types?''

''That is certain,'' I answered.

''And is it not, moreover, a provable thing that nothing can come from nothing, and that those lower types from which we here have evolved themselves evolved from lower yet, Nature being ever like herself? And though blood-crystals and serum-precipitates had not in that day heaved the simian descent of man from a theory to a scientific thesis, as a matter of fact was it not equally well known to thinkers at the date when Newman wrote?''

''Why, yes.''

"But Newman did not know it well? but continued to think of 'a terrible aboriginal calamity,' and of 'a world out of joint with the purposes of its Creator' — as if such things could be! — and of the 'tokens so faint and broken of design,' and of our race 'having no hope and being without God,' though, in truth, its hope begins to grow into a vision so glorified, that *'l'occhio da presso nol sostiene'?*"

"None of all that can be denied," I said.

"But, then, if this be so, shall we not say of Newman that his is a stubbornness become skittish, as it were of the frisking filly kicking up, for its part, its heels at the vague universe? For, if of a pair of statements, one that man rose slowly, the other that he fell suddenly, one practically proved and modern, its analogy everywhere to be noticed, the other not proved and ancient, its analogy nowhere to be noticed, and apparently foreign to Nature, Newman clung to the latter just because it was of the latter that his brain first caught an impression, 'when he was fifteen,' is not this a personally wayward playing at truth? and a thing rather disagreeably negroid? as the deaf adder stoppeth her ear? and will not hearken to the voice of charmers, charm they never so wisely, so Divinely?"

"Well, I consent," I said — "on this understanding, though, that Newman would have had an answer to all this, for he would have answered that intellect is weak, and reason rickety; that only that which Holy Writ and the Church assert is certainly true; and that this you will some day discover in hell, Monk."

"Well," said Monk, "at least one piece of that answer is most true, and let us say that the whole may be true — though, by the way, owing to my much greater greatness of mind, that is, my mental evolution, that is, my scepticism and proneness to truth, I know that it is not true in the same way that I know the untruth of the statements of negroes as regards corpses hurrying, or of Caesar as regards elks' legs, without even troubling to ask myself *how* I know. Still, let us say that this final reply of Newman may be true. Then, I say of it that it is precisely, to my knowledge, the final reply which a Barbados negro makes, without fail, to an opponent, my only care at present being to get you to agree that his Grace had a negroid brain."

"Well, let it be so," I said.

"But," he said, "having admitted that Newman had a mind which continued childish, you have admitted, I think, nothing which is at all likely to diminish your love of its charmingness. Here it seems, was a bud, not born to blow — because maybe the soil was thin? the air thick? — but still touched with that *mignon* endearment which the rose has outgrown: for to children and many immature things God does grant this special grace and engagingness, as Greek, gipsy, negro women exhibit a gracility which does not quite belong to the most evolved types; and the dayspring is prettier than the day."

"Yes, I see with you," I said, "and this talk of ours you should let me some day publish."

"I have no objection," he answered — "nay, it may do good: for let the man of Balham and of Birmingham once well learn the certainty of the truths which we have been proving, and Britain may then permanently disburden herself of her most just nervousness of Germany."

He Wakes an Echo

It seems incredible, but remember it was Regulus.—PLINY

We were down at the Abbey How, Monk's house in the Cotswolds, when Monk's weakness of the eyes — for which he wore a gold button in one ear — came upon him, and now he would cower for days over a library-grate, tamed, the green shade over his nose, his profile lighted by the fire. In fact our life was spent in the library, with every one of its procession of windows shuttered up, so that at midday we were as shut away from the sun as at midnight; and our consciousness that from outside the mansion had a look of having been deserted for ages may have confirmed our tendency to indolence, Monk giving hardly a sign of life, save an occasional shiver at the gales of autumn wawling all among the hills.

The reaction, however, in his case, was ever certain. A moment came when he stirred, and stretched; then for minutes a dead relapse; then a sitting forward with frowning thought, and now a spring up, a laugh, a mutter, "By Jingo, I'm hungry!"

For more things than one: for cities, and the storm of things, and the thick of war. At the same time he cast the shade from his eyes, and said to me: "Do you know what I have been thinking? That one of the big crimes would rouse and excite us."

"No doubt of that," I said: "but against whom shall we commit it?"

197

"Oh, come, one needn't go and commit it oneself," he said; "what I mean is that we should first conceive the crime, construct it, then find out someone who is somewhere committing it in the world, and mix ourselves up generally in the trouble."

"But in what possible way?" I asked, "and — with what earthly motive?"

"Isn't crime, being a human thing, my business?" he said.

"But — really, Monk — what sort of crime?"

"Crimes — that is what I have been thinking there — are of three sorts: little — usually heard of and punished; middle-sized — heard of, but not usually punished; and big — usually never heard of."

"But what do you call 'big' crimes?"

"Those which, like Borgia's, or Gilles de Rais's, are both large and dark-minded in mood; and 'little,' those which, like burglars' murders, are sordid in mood."

"But suppose there are no 'big crimes' going forward at present for us to 'mix ourselves up in'?"

"But isn't everything going forward that ever was or will be — doomsdays, moonfalls, cries of crucified Christs, rackets of Nile-cataracts, births of whirling worlds? As for our own sun, never before, credit me, did he blaze so crazily red, or so dreadfully roar on his road — what a bustle and thrill the whole thing is! Big crimes enough, I should think."

"Well, I am willing," I said, "though I like the light of day, and the pretty things that prink the sky at night, and have no wish to be shot. But how on earth — I can't even begin to conceive ——"

"Wait, we shall see; first, let's dine."

So we dined, and after dinner returned to the library where at once Monk, as he said, "set to work," first assuring me that there was no doubt about the result, since he had several methods in his head, and if one failed every one would not. And now he proceeded to spend three hours in a heat of activity, pitching up ladder-steps, eagerly dashing through leaves, with now a grumble, now a shrug, a mutter, hunting the rainbow, to "give to airy nothing a local habitation and a name."

I saw him pry into A B C's, masses of Ordnance maps, through a shelf of old ledgers belonging to the insurance-branch of his house, piles of newspapers, books on science. At last he lit a cigar, cast himself down upon a couch, his arms behind his head, and laughed. It was then ten o'clock.

"Come," I said, "something has been discovered."

"Look you," Monk said, "since modern men by heredity and morals are given a bent against 'sin,' it is ever under some compelling temptation that they commit it. Well, but in temptation there are two elements — wish, possibility; so that, if I think of a 'sin' and desire to find out who is committing it, I commence by discovering those who have a roaring opportunity for doing so. Now, suppose I conceive that someone wants, for any reason, to lure a stranger or so into his clutches, what are the ideal conditions as to 'opportunity' which I should seek? Those conditions occur in the case of a man living near one of two very obscure railway-stations which have nearly the same name: so I found out the sixteen such pairs of stations which exist in Europe, and wrote them down — one such pair, I may tell you at once, being Stratton Eastern and Stratton Western in Scotland. Very good. Now, suppose on discovering this fact, I discover also this constantly repeated advertisement: 'Summerdale Farm. Paying guests received. Every home comfort. Climate highly recommended by the Profession. Terms moderate. Near Stratton Western, Kincardine. — Apply J. P., "Telegraph," Box No. 3715.' And suppose I moreover discover, firstly, that this climate, so highly recommended by the Profession, is the climate of a storm-swept coast, almost uninhabited; and secondly, that there is no record anywhere of any such farm in Kincardine as Summerdale Farm?''

''That might be ugly,'' I agreed.

''You see, of course,'' he went on, ''what might very well happen to a 'paying guest' who starts to get to 'Summerdale Farm.' His friends, if he has any, know that he has gone to Stratton Western; his train arrives, let us say, one evening at Stratton Western; his luggage is put upon the local cab, if there is one — upon some species of thing with wheels — and now he gives the order 'Summerdale Farm.' However, his driver knows no Summerdale Farm — no one knows it — it doesn't, in fact, exist. But at last the idea inevitably strikes someone that the stranger has made a mistake — that the farm must be at Stratton Eastern, not at Stratton Western; and, sure at first though our stranger is that Western it is, and not Eastern, finally, in his perplexity, and hunger, maybe, he is tempted to try Eastern, whither by the next train he goes. Here someone — maybe disguised — awaits him with a trap. 'Is he not the stranger expected at Summerdale Farm?' Yes. He enters that trap; and a trap it proves. He is driven a long way, perhaps, to a place which is not Summerdale Farm, and no trace from that moment remains of that man in this world.''

''Well!'' I exclaimed.

"Unless, indeed, the evil-doer has the imprudence to compromise himself by taking out a rather unusual number of policies of insurance ——"

"No! *Is* there someone at Stratton Eastern who has done that?"

"Not very far from Stratton Eastern — a certain Sir Saul Ingram, as I see, residing at Feuding Manor, thereabouts. Far be it from me to assert that this good Sir Saul, who has taken out the policies, and the man who has advertised the fictitious farm are the same. Still, I have a greed on me to see this Feuding Manor, and I mean to go to it."

"Not alone?"

"Yes, since I have a sort of guess in my head that Sir Saul Ingram may be a country squire of unquiet type, and you have said that you like the sun."

His eye twinkled, but his tone was decided. I did not know what to say; and when I woke the next morning my Monk had already taken train northward. At nine the same evening (as it was related to me afterwards) he arrived at Stratton Eastern.

There, after making a good many inquiries, he got to hear something of the whereabouts of Feuding Manor, miles away, and set off on foot over a tract of "links" — sand-dunes mixed with scrub — where the solitude was absolute. Great guns of wind were blowing a roar of breakers shoreward from over a dark sea chill with waters from the North Pole — a storm with something in its tone which seemed to Monk to mean that here it was no occasional comer, but the everlasting master of that coast. Warned as he had been in regard to the quicksands near the seaboard of the links, and hearing the roar of breakers grow in his ears, as he dug his way head-foremost in the teeth of the gale, he was directing his course more westward, when a great gust tugged his hat from his hands and head, and carted it into the dark. With the wind now at his right shoulder, he went on hatless for some forty minutes, till he found the ground begin to harden; and soon he was following a footpath through a wood of alders that presently thickened to a forest where he could scarcely see his hand, and then anew thinned to a wood, through which he passed downwards by a path, and now found himself in a vale, enclosed by fells and scars; and he could make out before him a lake of water.

He thought that this ought to be the place; but, as he could make out nothing with any distinctness, he stood in uncertainty a little, until up burned the brim of the moon luridly above a scar; and now he could perceive the shape of a house, darksome, low, and large, on an ait or island, lying in a lowland mere.

Not one blink of light came out from it; but, without hesitation, Monk walked down to the edge of the mere, found a causeway of stone leading to the island; went over it; passed at the end of it between two rocks like druidical ''standing-stones,'' and, sending a flock of black-faced sheep bleating away through bracken, began to prowl round the grounds and house.

The ground he found very rough, without any visible road; the alders and willows huddled all one way by the continual sea-storm; and, as to the house, its structure was most intricate and quaint, the roofs of different breadths, spouts out of the straight, with an outhouse or lean-to here or there. But what struck him was the apparently hoary age of the whole, the walls being propped with beams which were themselves watery and soft with rot; and here or there a mass of masonry and beams had tumbled. Every window on both stories was boarded up; and, though Monk again and again glued his eyes to the boardings, he was able to spy no glimmer of light. All of a sudden a muffled, yet wild, howl wawled out of the house.

Plan of action Monk had as yet none: yet upon action of some sort he was resolved; and hearing, as he now stood thinking how he was to act, a horse's neigh, he followed the sound, and came to an outhouse in an alder-spinney. This proved to be a stable, and there, against the door, stood a spade, a rake, and a crowbar.

Monk took the crowbar and with it returned to the house, where, after scrambling to the roof of a low lean-to, he set to work upon a window shuttered by a sheet of iron just over the roof, the loud roar of the winds drowning the sounds of his fumbling. The roof, being mossy, was very slippery; but, lying along it, he managed presently to prise open the iron slab, which yielded with a pop, though, as it turned out, the wrench did not break the catch: this lacked a handle, and when Monk had drawn the shutter towards him against the force of the storm, and had sprung into the apartment beyond, the wind again slammed the shutter, he heard the catch click, and realized that he was a prisoner.

Light though his leap was, it shook the house, which he felt shake throughout to each gust of the gale, and here, it was clear, was the home of old decay. As he stood there in a darkness that was complete, from somewhere far away there came to his ears a cry like the wail of one rived with pain; and when upon this Monk struck a match, there, at his feet, kneeling with a face of fear, he saw a man, quite young, yet with long, white hair, clad in the rags of a dressing-gown.

Monk, having struck another match, put his left hand on the lad's head, murmuring to him: "I am not going to hurt you; do I look, now, as if I would? Tell me who you are."

Nothing but a species of jabbering proceeded in answer out of the throat of the lad, who, opening his mouth wide, pointed inward to it.

"Ah!" said Monk, when he saw that the lad had no tongue. And he kept on striking matches, examining that prostrate shape, examining the chamber.

He saw that there were two truckle-beds, from one of which the lad had apparently just risen, the other being "made"; and at the foot of this other — chained to it — was a cash-box, which Monk was going to investigate when the lad held him back with a grip and gaze of warning — a gaze that all at once grew aghast at a sound of footsteps coming without. Quickly now Monk struck another match, hustled the lad into a large cupboard, without shelves, in a corner, locked its door upon him, kept the key; then, flying to the lad's bed, with that lightning knack of which he, above all mortals, was a master, so arranged the bedclothes as to lend them an air of covering a slumberer. An instant later the key turned in the lock and there entered a very bulky man, bearing a candlestick with a tallow candle stuck in it. Monk, though he had purposely come to this house without a weapon, boldly faced him.

The man, dressed in a loose red shirt which bagged over his girdle, was evidently a servant, had an expression of dullness and grimness, a great fan-beard, and eyes nearly invisible beneath their lax lids, that resembled little draperies of skin. At sight of Monk his conduct was extraordinary. He simply dropped candlestick and candle, dashed to the cash-box, and, hugging it with both arms, began to bawl ''Help!'' But in one half-minute his mood of miserly affright changed into hatred; he bounded towards a stool and caught and swung it to dash out Monk's brains, but Monk made a dodge as if to seize the cash-box, and the man, seeing this in the still-burning candlelight, bounded to intercept him; upon which Monk dived and escaped out of the chamber.

Monk, after first leaving the crowbar in a corner and marking the spot in his mind, darted onward, little knowing whither, through the most curious old house which he had yet seen, where one chamber was higher or lower than the next by three or four steps, where nothing appeared quite straight, and doors hung awry, and the very floors were aslant. He went butting into triangular rooms, antic nooks, whimsical corners, till, at last, seeing a blink of light ahead, he boldly moved towards it, opened a door, and entered a room.

As he stepped in there hastened to meet him — a man; and both stood stone-still, and looked at each other.

The man — a powerful person of middle height — walked with a busy fling-out of the right leg, and with his left hand stuck in the pocket of his robe, which was tied with a cord round the waist. He wore spectacles across his broad face, and had a broad mouth and an out-sticking, stiff beard, so hairy as even to invade the fat of his cheeks.

At last he spoke, saying quite coolly —

''Well, you silly devil, what are you doing here?''

His speech was a species of rapid mutter, and even in the act of speaking, his tongue-tip was ever out, seeking for one end of his moustache to eat.

''I am here to find a brother of mine,'' answered Monk.

''What name?''

"Never mind his name. The lad whose tongue you have cut out, Sir Saul Ingram."

"Same father? Same mother?"

"Adam and Eve, you know."

"Silly devil!" muttered the man musingly.

Now, during this talk Monk had stood with his palms pressed on the round table in the middle of the room, his back towards the one door; and the baronet, who was more remote from the door, had been moving round towards it — a movement that Monk did not fail to notice, though he made no attempt to stop it. So now, with a sudden run, Ingram gained the door, closed it, locked it. He then stepped to a small chest of drawers, caught up out of one of the drawers a revolver, turned anew upon his prisoner, and now his mouth drew back in a sort of snarl that resembled a laugh.

"What you do it for?" he asked Monk, with the breadth of the table between them, and his laugh had something strained in it, cruel and hard to see, as though done by machinery which lacked oil.

"Are you going to shoot me," asked Monk — "an unarmed and helpless man?"

"Silly devil!" muttered Ingram, almost laughing out now, "of course I'm going to! What you do it for?"

"I have help near; I defy you to shoot."

"Pooh! Lie!"

"I have!"

"Lie! Look out!" He raised and aimed the weapon; his finger rested on the trigger.

All the house trembled with many a weary creak to the power of the storm, while four or five seconds passed, in which the baronet appeared to be enjoying a consciousness of power before firing. The shot, however, was never fired. Instead of it there rang out a passionate shout — from outside the house, apparently —a cry in the night: "Monk! Monk! I'll be here for you at two with the police!"

It was the baronet who seemed shot. He fell back some feet, rushed aimlessly to the door, aimlessly back again, gaping in a frank scare, realizing no doubt that, if Monk's presence in the house was known outside it, then Monk's death, and the manner of it, was a matter for reflection. But in a minute he was partially reassured by Monk himself, who said to him: "Look you, you were right; I have no help near, for that shout came from *me*, and only seemed to come from outside because I chance to be the sort of man who can do such things. But you see now, don't you, Ingram, if you are not a goose, that I wasn't altogether fashioned to be shot down by a clown like you? You couldn't, really. Try again, and I have five other ways of stopping you, some of them not so agreeable. Better keep quiet."

Ingram eyed Monk with a grim underlook, quite undecided now, no doubt, as Monk wished him to be, which was the untruth — whether the cry had or had not come from outside. After a minute of thought, he turned away, inwardly resolving, perhaps, to wait till two, the hour mentioned by the voice that had appeared to shout from outside. After two — he would see.

It was at this point that a rap sounded on the locked door, and when Ingram opened it, there slouched in the big man in the loose red shirt whom Monk had encountered before; he bore dishes on both his palms, and was followed by a tall woman of a visage most white and gaunt, with jaundiced eye-whites, robed in a gown of rusty black, who bore on a tray a bottle, a plate, and a tablecloth. The man took not the slightest notice of Monk, but the woman eyed him curiously, with a look of rancor. No one spoke. The woman spread the table with the tablecloth, the man put on the dishes. But as she turned to go, the woman, holding up a finger, said to Ingram: "Saul, mon, Saul, gi' heed! There be danger this nicht!"

The baronet made no answer, locked the door after them, and sat to a repast of potatoes, boiled cod, bread black as coal, whisky-and-water; and he began to eat with a greedy earnestness and to drink.

After some minutes he glanced up at Monk, who stood regarding him with folded arms, and said: "Sit down, if you like."

Monk sat on a chair by the table, watching for some time the guzzling of Ingram, watching the revolver at his right hand on the table, watching the great gulps of whisky which the man — who ate and drank more like a yokel than a gentleman — imbibed. At last, yielding, perhaps, to the garrulous influence of a third whisky, Ingram suddenly said: "Silly devil! What you do it for?"

"Do what?" asked Monk.

"What you come here for?"

"I found out that you were up to some kind of mischief, and came to stop you."

"Mischief — eh? Know what I am?"

"No. Tell me."

"I am the only exact scientist in the world."

"Oh, come, not the only one."

"See those three big books here on the shelf? They are all in manuscript. I wrote them. Going to burn them before I die.

Almost the whole secret of body and soul is in them — the secret of life.''

''By Jove! And by what methods?''

''There's only one way — persistent human vivisection.''

''By Jove!''

The baronet's words for a moment seemed to burn Monk's brain, which was yet no stranger to notions of horror; but here was something new to him: and he gaped with a grain of something resembling reverence at that greasy, plump face, as Ingram drained yet another glass.

''Know what I shall probably do with you?'' said the baronet. ''Good thing you came. Infect you with a culture of rabid germs which I have on hand, then vivisect, perhaps, if I have time. The dumb fellow you saw — young parson from Cambridge — am driving mad for sake of living brain. Doctors say, you know, that they can't discover any morbid anatomy in mad brains. Silly devils! No morbid anatomy! Oh, good Lord! Silly devils!''

Ingram grinned sweetly to himself at this, grovelling with a full mouth over his meal.

''But how on earth do you drive people mad?'' asked Monk.

''Fear, torture, horror, chiefly. Other things, too; have eighty-eight snakes, one jaguar, and a monster grouse with four legs in the house. Simple solitary confinement sometimes. Depends on diathesis of patient.''

''Well, you are candid enough,'' said Monk. ''How if friends are really coming to rescue me at two? I'll naturally repeat all this.''

''No, you don't, friends or no friends. Suppose I wanted to hide you from them — alive — on the premises, think I couldn't? Why, I have seventeen people here now, undergoing various preparations, and you might search as you choose, you wouldn't find one. A man like me can devise a sure hiding place, I suppose?''

"If you hid me, I should call out, of course."

"Not much you wouldn't. I could strike you dumb in three minutes without leaving a sign to show how. But you won't be here to call out. Know what I mean to do with you? Did it once before eight years ago, and once again four years ago. Put your dead body in a packing-case with gun-cotton and a time-fuse, send you off in first goods train, and thirty miles from Stratton Eastern scarcely a trace left of you, or of the van that carried you.''

"I see," said Monk. "But, even so, you won't escape the law, for one of my friends knows of the presence here of the dumb lad, who will be looked for, and undoubtedly found, however you may conceal him.''

"Found, will he? Your statement that someone knows that he is here, whether true or false, merely decides me to examine his brain tonight, instead of next week.''

"Still, traces of the body will be found.''

"Traces, no. His body will go with yours in the packing-case to the railway.''

"I see — I see. But tell me one thing — since science is your motive for trapping strangers into this house, how comes it that your name figures in insurance policies?''

Ingram at this glanced up angrily, stung in his honor, crying — "What! You know of that? And do you suppose that the motives of a lord of thought, of a man like me, could be tainted in that sordid way? Why, I live on about sixpence a day — except the whisky; and if I didn't have the sixpence, I'd do without. Sometimes I do take out a policy on a patient, but the money doesn't come to *me*, silly devil! I've got two misers in the house, that's all — Hubert and my sister, whom you saw just now — and I get the money to give to them, in the hope that they'll tear each other to shreds over it. Beastly misers! That man Hubert — miserly beast, murderous beast! Mad as a mad dog! Silly devil, thinks I am forever on the look-out to steal the very money I have given him! Sleeps in the same room as fellow without tongue and no human being dare approach room a single moment. Once wanted to do for me. Mad dog!''

''I see,'' said Monk. ''But is it your whisky, or what, that has made you so very candid? Doesn't it really occur to you, Ingram, that with the knowledge that you have now given me of yourself I could snuff you out without fail in five or six different ways, without lifting a finger? Could make you commit suicide, for example? or make Hubert kill you? or your sister kill you? or make you all kill one another in a mix-up? And, considering how gory a thing, Ingram, you have allowed yourself to grow into, I do here and now deliberately pass sentence of death upon you. You really shan't live through this night, I vow, you wretch!''

The baronet did not even give an upward glance at this threat, believing, maybe, that here was a diseased brain come spontaneously for his scalpel. The rude repast concluded, he now picked his teeth musingly, while a clock struck midnight; and always outside wailed the storm.

''Hubert!'' presently roared the baronet, at the same time clattering a huge bell.

And now anew came Hubert slouching in.

"Look," the baronet said to him, "in the dissecting-room closet, and carry the top one of those three long boxes to your room. Dumb Wilson and this man have got to go into it, and you've got to take them to the station at five in the morning. Understand?"

Hubert made a sound not unlike the grunt of a pig.

"And don't go holding matches and things over the box, now, silly devil!" said Ingram, grinning one of his grim smiles: "it's got gun-cotton in it."

Hubert grunted, but did not move.

"Well, why don't you go?" asked Ingram.

"Why must the box be e'en stowed in *my* room?" asked Hubert.

"Oh, go away, you, and do what I tell you!" said the baronet. "Who the deuce wants to steal your daft money? I'm not even going to enter your room!"

Hubert grunted, reassured, and went out. And now Ingram at once began to make his preparations for the investigation of the dumb lad's brain, taking two instrument-cases from a bureau, examining three scalpels, a trephine, and a saw, one by one, over the lamp, and laying them side by side on the sill of a window, each of the three scalpels being wrapped in a piece of chamois leather. The dim room was crowded all round with shelves, on which stood hundreds of chemical jars, and, like all the house, was pervaded with a breath of the laboratory, a scent of research, and also a certain taint of death. The baronet had just laid down the instruments side by side on the window-seat, when a face with jaundiced eyes peeped in, saying: "Saul, mon, I wad ha' speech wi' ye."

The baronet stalked to her, and, while a little outside the door they stood talking, Monk stole close and hearkened.

"Saul, mon," the woman said, "'tis no ower weel this nicht, I'm doubting. I hae heard your talk wi' yon callant ——"

"Well, what's the matter now, Elspeth?" asked the baronet impatiently.

"Are ye minded to mak' only mair operations on Wilson to-nicht, Saul?" she asked. "Tak' a fule's counsel, and no do it, for 'tis e'en a long wark, and ye wad no hae the time."

"Why can't you be quiet? What is it you want with me?" asked the baronet.

"Split Wilson's throat at once like a heather-blutter's, Saul," she answered, "and yon callant's, too, and pit them baith tegither into the box for the station. Tak' a fule's counsel, for I feel a sair fricht, mon, on me. Ye canna hae the time for mair long operations, for ye kenna what aid this man may e'en ha' outside; and here is Hubert threeping that one o' the dangerous snakes has escaped, and I near swafing awa' wi' fright ——"

Monk, his whole plan of action now decided upon, stopped to listen to no more; but, moving from the door, flew lightly round the crowded shelves, searching till he found a bottle marked "Phosphorus," which contained some waxy, semi-transparent sticks in water. This he took down, and took out one of the phosphorus sticks, first throwing some of the cold water on his fingers so that their warmth should not cause the phosphorus to break into flame; and now, running to the window-sill, he took one of the three scalpels which lay there out of its chamois leather wrapping, made the inner fold of the leather damp with some water to keep it cold for some minutes at least, and then, putting the stick of phosphorous with the scalpel, wrapped it up anew. He had barely put back the bottle in its place when the baronet came in again, stalked to the window, hurriedly put all the rolls of leather into an outer pocket of his robe, phosphorus and all, and set to calling out "Hubert!"

"Look you," said Monk, now frowning balefully, "let me save you some trouble, sir. You are now calling this Hubert, I think, in order to send him for the dumb lad, whom you desire to be taken to your dissecting-room. Well, I say now to you that the lad is gone — has escaped — is at this moment free ——"

Ingram turned quite white.

"What are you saying?" he asked.

"He is gone, I tell you. If you don't believe me, go and see. I set him at liberty myself."

At those words the baronet flew. To this moment the disappearance of Wilson had not been discovered, probably owing to Monk's lifelike placing of the bedclothes when he had locked away the dumb lad in the cupboard. At any rate, so intense was the baronet's care at this ugly news that he even forgot to lock Monk in — only for one instant, indeed, for he flew back, transferred the key from the inside to the outside, turned it, then in wild flight was off anew, making for Wilson's chamber — which was Hubert's, too; and he was just off when Hubert, in answer to his summons, turned the key, entered, and was looking round to see the baronet, who had called him, when Monk burst out laughing.

"Why, whom are you looking for?" asked Monk. "Not the baronet, surely? Tut, man! Where's your head? He only called you to get you out of the way while he went into your room. He told you just now that he wasn't going there at all, didn't he?

Well, but as a man of the world, you can easily guess that he's in want of a little ready cash tonight, of all nights, to buy my silence. Take my advice: lie low — say nothing.''

At these words the man's face passed through all the expressions of disbelief, belief, rage, lunacy; and suddenly, casting up his arms, he took to his heels. Monk had the hope that in the man's access of miserly fright he would omit to lock the door in his flight, and he did; but, after one moment's forgetfulness, he, too, darted back to the key, turned it, and was away again.

Monk, then, was still a prisoner; but he now no sooner found himself alone than he began to shout, in a perfect imitation of Ingram's voice: ''Hi! Elspeth! Elspeth!'' and when in a minute the baronet's sister peeped in, looking keenly round for her brother, Monk, bowing, said to her: ''The baronet has just left the room, madam. I see that he is in a great hurry to make his experiment on the dumb lad, and is now gone to get all ready; but, hurry as he may, I tell you that he will hardly have time. Look you, will you make a bargain with me?''

''Weel?'' asked Elspeth, with a crafty twitching of the cheeks and eyes.

''Madam,'' said Monk, ''I stand this night in a huge danger; but so do you: and if I show you how to save yourself, will you save me? Is that a bargain?''

''Ye-es,'' said the woman.

''Well, I'll tell you. In one half-hour my friends will be here, and as they have reason to believe that Wilson is here, the only hope for you really is to have Wilson out of the house in the box before they come; but, since the baronet is bent upon his experiment on Wilson, and won't give it up, there seems really nothing for you to do but to destroy the lad with your own hands now — this moment — as he lies a-bed, before the baronet can get him for the experiment; for the baronet will have no use for the dead body, it is the living brain that he is bent on studying. So now I have told you how to act, will you save my life in return?''

''We'll e'en see,'' answered Elspeth, with twitching eyes of craft; but she saw fully the force of Monk's remarks, which accorded with her own views — saw that Wilson must, in truth, die by her hands, since by no other. And at once making up her mind, she turned to the bureau, unlocked a drawer by one of the bundle of keys at her girdle, and drew forth a horn-handled dagger, her purpose, as Monk well knew, being to spring first upon him, stab him, and then hurry to the dumb lad's bedside. But while she was still stooping over the bureau, Monk had caught up Ingram's water-jug, which was still half-full of water, and had hidden it behind his back, at the same time looking down at the floor, which he found to slant somewhat, like many of the floors of the house; and as the woman was in the act of raising herself to turn upon him, there hissed forth between Monk's teeth the two words: ''A snake!''

''A snake!''

Elspeth glared with panic where he pointed, and her glance saw in the gloom a wiry form gliding over the floor towards her — a snake created by Monk, who, having previously heard her say that one of the baronet's poison-snakes had escaped, had now, out of the water-bottle held behind his back, poured an undulating rivulet over the floor. The woman flew; and, as she flew, again glanced backward, only once more to behold the infuriated pursuit of the snake over the slanting floor; nor gave she

any third glance, but — serpents being clearly her weak point —
sent throughout the house a shriek, and was gone, leaving the
door open, Monk after her, tracking the sound of her footfalls,
himself all unmarked, through the vast intricacies of that house
which held so many ghastly secrets, towards Wilson's apartment.

The situation at that moment in the room of Wilson, Monk
declares that he knew with a precision almost as absolute as
though he saw it. He had sent the baronet to search for Wilson,
and he had sent the miser Hubert to search for the baronet.
Now, Monk was certain that Ingram had a real fear of Hubert's
growls and miserly furies, and he knew that no sooner would
Ingram have discovered the absence of Wilson than he would
hear the oncoming of the snorts and wrathful grunts of Hubert;
upon which it was certain that the baronet, to avoid a scene, or
something worse, would wish to secrete himself. But Monk
knew that there was absolutely no hiding-place in that room,
save two — the cupboard, and the rumpled bedclothes of
Wilson's truckle-bed. The cupboard, containing Wilson, Monk
had locked. It was natural, therefore, that Ingram, knowing that
Hubert was still ignorant of the disappearance of Wilson, would
scuttle well beneath Wilson's bedclothes, and pretend to be
Wilson asleep. And Monk had now effectually prompted Elspeth
to the murder of Wilson in his bed; provided she did which
quickly and quietly, it was sure as doom she would stab her
brother.

Something more or less corresponding to these calculations
must really have taken place. Hubert, on entering Wilson's
room, must have struck a match, stared round, observed no

baronet there, and now, perhaps, was about to go out again, when he must have heard footsteps — the footsteps of Elspeth coming to kill Wilson. Hubert's miserly suspicions must at once anew have burst into bloom, and he must have crouched down somewhere to watch what would take place. Elspeth then went in, Monk by that time being close behind her, though before he could reach the door, she had shut and secured it; and he stood keenly listening outside. And now the woman, moving no doubt on hands and knees, steel in hand, in the deep darkness crawled for the bed on which lay her brother, the supposed Wilson: for suddenly — short, but most raucous — Monk heard the outburst of a shout.

At this outcry of the murdered baronet, Hubert most likely leapt up: for presently Monk heard Elspeth explaining to him her motive for disposing at once of the dumb lad; and this was followed by a noise of shuffling feet when the body was being raised and placed in a packing-case, which was waiting there to receive the remains of Monk and Wilson. The garment worn by Wilson was of the same sort as that worn by Ingram, and no suspicion of the truth could have occurred to the criminals, who were sufficiently well advised to strike no matches over the gun-cotton in that box; and Monk heard the drop of the lid over the deposited body.

And now he knew that there was need for haste. In the box was gun-cotton, and in the baronet's pocket was a piece of phosphorus, for Monk, who could be ruthless, had doomed all the three. That phosphorus must quickly fire at the warmth of a still-warm body packed into that confined space, the moistened chamois-leather which wrapped it round being now nearly dry.

Now, therefore, to the spot where he had deposited the crowbar Monk darted, then back again to the room; outside which, at about the spot where the cupboard which contained Wilson stood, he began to dig deeply at the oak boarding with heavy heaves of the body. Within, Elspeth and Hubert must have hearkened with a paralysis of awe to those earnest strokes of the crowbar, to that breath of Monk's breast, while on he toiled in the momentary expectancy of death, till at last the oak was cracking, a plank splintered, another, and an opening was there. Monk put in his hand, felt the contact of chilly flesh, dragged the lad out, tossed the meager form over his shoulders, and now, as though the fiend was after him, went flying, with many a blind stumble and fumble about the house. Wilson's arm clasped his neck, almost choking him, and from the dumb throat moaned a whimpering; while Monk, gasping beneath his load, roamed onward in random trepidation, till, spying a gleam like moonshine through a crack, he again and again drove his back against some boarding, tumbled outward, and, by a drop down of fifteen feet, was rolling in bracken.

Catching up Wilson afresh, Monk now made paces from the house; and had not run thirty yards, when behind him a disturbance like the bursting of some tremendous drum had the earth atremble; whereupon Monk, glancing backward, saw, like startled grouse in the midst of a spout of glare, a swarm of débris flying. Then followed three more brisk bangs; and the explosion, which was quite local to Wilson's room, was over. But some instinct of general ruin held Monk rooted where he stood during two full minutes of dreadful expectation; at the end of which, at a point not very remote from the place of the explosion, a case of masonry disengaged itself from the house, and thumped in powder to the ground; there came a greater rage of the gale; the house seemed to totter to its downfall; a larger wall of mason-work tumbled outward in a smoke of dust; from the interior there pealed forth, joined in one choir a shriek of many voices; and a moment later the whole area of the mansion nodded, roared, and hastily rushed into ruin. On Monk's breast lay the dumb lad sobbing.